THE MESMERIST

RONALD L. SMITH

CLARION BOOKS
HOUGHTON MIFFLIN HARCOURT
BOSTON   NEW YORK

Clarion Books
3 Park Avenue
New York, New York 10016

The text was set in Freight Text Pro.
Book design by Lisa Vega

Library of Congress Cataloging-in-Publication Data
Names: Smith, Ronald L. (Ronald Lenard), 1959– author.
Title: The mesmerist / Ronald L. Smith.
Description: Boston ; New York : Clarion Books, Houghton Mifflin Harcourt, 2017.
| Summary: "Thirteen-year-old Jess and her mother make a living as sham
spiritualists—until they discover that Jess is a mesmerist and that she really can talk
to the dead. Soon she is plunged into the dark world of Victorian London's supernatural
underbelly and learns that the city is under attack by ghouls, monsters, and spirit
summoners"—Provided by publisher.
Identifiers: LCCN 2016016162 | ISBN 9780544445284 (hardback)
Subjects: | CYAC: Supernatural—Fiction. | Occultism—Fiction. |
Good and evil—Fiction. | Identity—Fiction. | London (England)—History—19th
century—Fiction. | Great Britain—History—Victoria, 1837-1901—Fiction. | BISAC:
JUVENILE FICTION / Horror & Ghost Stories. | JUVENILE FICTION / Historical /
Europe. | JUVENILE FICTION / Lifestyles / City & Town Life. | JUVENILE FICTION /
Visionary & Metaphysical.
Classification: LCC PZ7.1.S655 Me 2017 | DDC [Fic]—dc23
LC record available at https://lccn.loc.gov/2016016162

Manufactured in the United States of America
DOC 10 9 8 7 6 5 4 3 2 1
4500636782

For Margot and Fafi

Contents

Contents

THE MESMERIST

PART ONE

The Girl in the Wardrobe

CHAPTER ONE

England, 1864

A Thousand Shards of Porcelain

Being stuffed into a wardrobe with your hands tied is a dreadful way to start your day.

There's hardly any light, but for the yellow glint of a candle flame through a small crack in the door. Dust tickles my nostrils. Spiders are in the corners too.

I hate spiders.

I breathe out through my nose and try to think of something peaceful—something besides Dr. Barnes sitting with Mother, nervously clutching a handkerchief or glass of sherry, hoping beyond hope that somehow, a message from his dead daughter, Lydia, will be revealed.

That would be through me.

I am the vessel, you see, through which the dead loved one will speak.

Actually, it is all a sham.

This is how it works.

We knew Dr. Barnes had lost his daughter recently, and when he made the appointment, all it took was a few flowery words to begin the ruse:

Dear Papa,
Dab your eyes, dry your tears.
I am in the bosom of the Lord,
in Whose grace I have found
everlasting peace.
Yours always,
Lydia.

What Dr. Barnes doesn't know is that an hour before his arrival, I wrote this very message on a chalk slate and hid it in the wardrobe's secret panel. From there, it became a very simple matter to step inside with a blank one and make the swap. Also—and this is key—Mother is very good at tying slipknots.

Soft murmurs echo beyond the door. I picture Mother with closed eyes, her thin nostrils flaring. On some days, the flames from the fireplace provide enough heat for her face to flush, which makes the act all the more authentic.

I hear the scrape of a chair and then footsteps. *Finally.* I sigh in relief. I want to get out of here.

I pinch my cheeks for a rosy flush and slip my hands back into the knot. The iron lock of the wardrobe clicks. The door squeaks open. I take a deep breath, force my body to go limp, and then, with an exaggerated gasp, fall face forward onto the floor.

Dr. Barnes leaps out of his chair. I hear his teacup rattle on the table and then crash, sending a thousand shards of porcelain across the brick tiles of the hearth. "Oh, my God!" he cries. "Is she . . . is she dead?"

Mother, being a true professional, plays her part with ease. "No, she is fine. She has been to the other side. Please. Give her a moment."

She kneels and leans in close, then brushes a lock of hair from my eyes. The fresh scent of Cameo Rose surrounds me. It is a lovely fragrance, and one I always associate with Mother, which lifts my spirits whenever I am down—something I feel at this very moment, for I can already feel the bruise swelling on my forehead. She helps me up, unties the thin rope that binds my wrists, and leads me to a long chaise covered in red and blue damask. Dr. Barnes, old chap, withdraws a silk handkerchief from his vest pocket. "There, there, dear girl," he says, dabbing my brow. I almost feel sorry for him. I ease my head back and let out a breath.

Mother picks up the slate from the floor. She gives Dr. Barnes a sharp look. "The dead do not always speak what we would wish to hear," she intones. "And oftentimes, their messages can be confusing . . . or even incomprehensible."

Dr. Barnes exhales a shaky breath. Mother unclasps the two sides of the slate.

The blood drains from her face.

"What is it?" Dr. Barnes asks, drawing closer.

Mother is speechless, her mouth open in shock or confusion, I don't know which.

Dr. Barnes wrenches the slate away and peers over the top of his spectacles. I sit up and read the words written in a crooked script.

Ring around the rosy, a pocketful of posies.
Ashes! Ashes! We all fall down!

And below, written in a spidery scrawl, one single letter . . .

M

CHAPTER TWO

To London

A bead of sweat trembles on Dr. Barnes's bulbous nose. "Dear God," he cries. "What is this? My Lydia. Where is she? Where is my sweet child?"

I look to Mother, still standing, but she is motionless, as if struck dumb.

A sudden chill settles over me, even though the fire is blazing.

Ashes! Ashes! We all fall down!

I did not write these words.

"We must investigate," I inform Dr. Barnes, trying to keep my composure.

Truth be told, I am just as shocked as he is.

I stand up and gently nudge him out the door with quiet, consoling words, then walk back in and carefully step over the broken bits of porcelain. Mother has taken a seat on the chaise. Her face is drawn, her green eyes cold and far away.

"What happened?" I ask, standing before her. "How did that message get there?"

No answer.

"Mother, have you taken ill?"

"This is . . . I must—I need time to think, Jessamine."

She's hiding something. Mother never hides anything from me.

"Who is M?" I venture. "Who . . . who wrote that on the slate?"

She stands up and smoothes her wool soutache jacket with her palms, then slowly walks to the mahogany sideboard, where alcoholic spirits are displayed in heavy crystal decanters. A glass chimes as she takes one down from the cabinet. The pungent scent of anisette and fennel fills the room. I love the smell of absinthe. It reminds me of black licorice at Christmastime with Father, but since his death, I believe Mother drinks the "Green Faerie" a little too often.

She turns around, her eyes suddenly a little less far away.

"We must travel to London," she says. "There is someone there who can give us answers."

"London?" I ask. I was born there and remained until the age of five, when Mother made our home here in Deal.

"Pack your things, dear," she tells me. "We must leave in the morning." She swallows the last of her drink.

For a moment, her shoulders slump, as if a great weight is bearing down upon her.

My shoes clack on the cobblestones, sending rats scurrying.

Someone is after me.

Who it is, I do not know. All I know is that I need to keep running.

My legs burn with fatigue and my breath comes in bursts. I need to rest. Just for a moment. Rest. That's what I need.

There—up ahead

The mouth of a narrow alley beckons. I dash the few short steps and take shelter, reaching out to the wall to steady myself. I feel something wet, rain perhaps. But as I raise my hand to my face, drifting night clouds reveal the moon, which illuminates what it truly is.

Blood.

My hand is covered in blood.

I look to the wall.

There, gleaming wet and bright, I see it:

M

I wake with a start, my breath caught in my throat. Early-morning sun leaks through the thin curtains. I'm safe—in my own room, at home. We will be traveling to London today.

The dream haunts my steps as I take the empty pitcher on my bedside table and head into the parlor. The room is cold and dark, and the greasy smell of tallow candles hangs in the air. I kneel before the fireplace and use a poker to stir up the coals. They are mostly cinders now, but a few are still in good condition, with just a corner of white ash, so I arrange them evenly and then add a few sticks of tinder. I light the wood with a match and watch as the small flame erupts and spreads quickly. Once the fire is going, I pour water into a pot that hangs suspended from a bar above the hearth. I have to do this every morning, and it is a laborious process.

At one time we had a maid-of-all-work, but since Father's death, that is a luxury we can no longer afford. The same goes for my schooling, which, I must admit, was not my favorite pastime anyway. Like many girls of my social class, I was taught at home by a governess. Mrs. Gillacuddy was her name, and she was absolutely dreadful. I once thought I saw her smile, but cannot be certain. It may have been indigestion.

I pour the hot water into a basin and carry it upstairs. I wash quickly—*Cleanliness is next to godliness*, the vicar often says—and then open the door to my wardrobe. A tremor of excitement runs through my veins. It is fleeting, however, as I soon remember our reason for traveling:

Ashes! Ashes! We all fall down!

What could it possibly mean?

I shake the thought away and ruffle through my clothing. I decide on an ivory-colored dress with lace and pearl buttons and an olive touring hat—one of my favorites, though I hardly ever have the chance to wear it. I finish the ensemble with a pair of brown button boots and a fur-collared cloak, which might come in handy, for the weather has become quite cool.

I turn to and fro before the standing mirror—the perfect image of a middle-class young lady. At least that's what Mother would say. *We must keep up appearances,* she often tells me, and does everything in her power to make that so.

Mother.

When I think of her, my heart blooms with love, even though we have certainly had our disagreements. What she has been through is a testament to her strength. Father died of consumption when I was five years old. He left us a small inheritance, but after a few years the money dwindled, and Mother said she was sure we were headed for the workhouse. That was when, with a very keen sense of timing, she decided to put out a shingle and take up our trade in the practice of spiritualism, a movement made all the more popular by the Russian immigrant Madame Blavatsky, who has become a guest and confidante to some of the most distinguished names of the day. We hold séances and read fortunes, ruminate over tea leaves, perform acts of levitation—which is really nothing but a parlor trick—and we even once contacted the spirit of a tabby cat called Finikin. *Allegedly.*

People come from far and wide to witness firsthand the uncanny talents of Cora Grace and Daughter. I fretted a little at the absence of my name at first, but Mother said it was quite pleasing to the ear.

Most of our clients are from the upper class and have more than enough money to see them through till the end of their days. If it gives them comfort to believe that their loved ones are at peace, so be it. But somewhere deep within me a spark of guilt flickers, no matter how hard I try to dampen it.

Downstairs, breakfast is laid out. Scones and Devonshire cream, toast, tea, and blackberry jam. Mother is already dressed and at the table. "We have a fairly long trip ahead of us," she says as I sit down. "I thought we should start with a proper breakfast."

We eat without saying much, and Mother still seems a little shaken. Her hands tremble as she raises the teacup to her lips.

"Who will we be meeting in London?" I ask.

"A man named Balthazar."

"Balthazar?" I venture. "What a strange name. And his surname?"

"Just Balthazar," she says vaguely. "He was a friend of Papa's."

I find this very odd. What could Father's friend have to do with what happened yesterday? Also, what kind of man deigns to go about without a surname? That, in my opinion, is the height of vanity.

After breakfast, Mother and I step out into the late-October morning. It is only a short walk to the station, and from there we will board the South Eastern Railway to London. My few belongings are packed in a lady's portmanteau, so it is not a bother to carry. The day is bright, and from where I stand, the English Channel unwinds like a long blue ribbon. A few herring gulls drift lazily on gusts of air, their wings spread wide, every now and then diving for a flash of silver. When I was a child, much to Mother's dismay, I spent hours at the docks watching the gulls, and making up imaginary stories filled with exotic animals and strange sea creatures. Only after hearing her call my name from afar would the spell be broken, and she would pull me away with a scolding. "There are dangerous men down there, Jessamine," she would say. "It is no place for a young lady."

I didn't find it dangerous. I found it thrilling—watching the ships come into port, the rough-looking men with their scruffy beards and strange voices. Often, I would play with an Indian girl named Deepa. She was lovely, with beautiful brown skin that did not burn in the sun, and long, dark eyelashes. Her father was an Englishman who traveled with the East India Company and one day brought home a wife. Unfortunately, because of Deepa's skin color, more times than once she would be set upon by some of the local boys, who called her dreadful names and chased her all the way home. I felt badly for her, but did not stand up to the ruffians. *What was I to do?* I was too small to have made any difference.

On one gray morning she met me at the dock with tears brimming in her eyes. She said that she and her mother would soon be taking the train to London to escape from her father, who had become besotted with drink. That was the last I saw of her, but to this day I think of her often.

Mother purchases tickets at the stationmaster's booth, and we wait on the wooden platform for the signal bell. It is a little cooler now, and I pull my cloak around my shoulders. A young boy strolls the platform, selling the latest newspapers from London, while uniformed porters stand waiting with passengers' bags and heavy trunks. After a moment I hear the whistle of the train, and a rush of air stirs the fabric of my dress. The sound of screeching wheels rings in my ears. The train comes to a grinding stop, and plumes of black smoke billow in the air. Mother and I head for the second-class coach. First class is beyond our means, and third, albeit cheaper, is recommended only for the poorest of the poor. It is not much more than an open box, with no protection from the elements. Thankfully, we have yet to fall that far.

We take a seat next to each other, and I place my bag above me in a net that holds newspapers and umbrellas. I pass the time gazing at the coastline through the cloudy window. Life is dull and unexciting where we live in Deal, in the South East of England. Our only claim to fame is that a few years earlier, pirates and smugglers plied their trade along the coast, shipping tobacco, wool, and other valuables across the Channel to France. In my flights of fancy as a child, I often wondered what it would be like to lead a criminal life, and even imagined myself as the heroine of my own tale: *The Adventures of Jess the Pirate Girl and her Deeds of Derring-Do!* Those memories are still dear to me, as Mother often played along while I ran about the house brandishing a carpet beater as a sword, laughter filling the halls. But after Father died, even though I was but a babe, our carefree playing ceased. Our maid was dismissed, and then my governess. Mother taught me lessons for a while, but soon, even that came to an end. Often, I would find her in the parlor at night, sitting by the light of the fire, staring into its flames as if she could find something there, if only she looked hard enough.

One night, she took me into her lap and cried, very quietly, as if she were pouring the grief out of her and into me. I took it all in and buried it down deep, where neither of us would ever have to find it again.

The ride to London is long, and the wooden bench is hard and uncomfortable. We should have brought cushions, I realize. We make several stops, the first being Canterbury, which leads to Ashford, then on to Tonbridge, Redhill, Croydon, and finally London. Mother takes out a deck of cards and we play a game of écarté, but neither one of us seems to give it her all.

After some time, the coastline gives way to green pastures and small rolling hills. A few brown fields and farms dot the landscape, and plumes of chimney smoke billow from solitary homes in the distance. A flock of birds wheels in the sky, and for some reason, a chill creeps across my bones.

I wake at the sound of the guard's booming voice. "Charing Cross station! Charing Cross is next!"

I sit up and knuckle my eyes. "I must have dozed off," I say, stifling a yawn.

"We're almost there," Mother says. "Next stop."

I look through the window. We are crossing a bridge, and

to either side, beyond the water, vast expanses of land are spread out, with patches of green here and there. Even from this distance, I can see great thoroughfares, and people as small as insects moving about.

"London," I say in amazement.

The train rumbles into a tunnel, and then there is darkness.

CHAPTER THREE

SummerHall

A circular roof of iron and glass looms above us. Late-afternoon light streams in and spills along the station floor. Long walls of brick on either side seem to go on forever.

I have never seen so many people in one place in my entire life.

They scurry to and fro, amidst black clouds of smoke belching from the hulking steel trains. Noise and activity is everywhere: the cries from newspaper boys and vendors of every sort, station attendants and passengers disembarking from the trains. It is a constant hum—a deep, echoing drone that does not let up for one moment.

"Where to now?" I ask Mother. She looks tired. I can see it in her eyes and the sag of her shoulders.

"Outside," she says, and I follow her through a doorway marked EXIT.

Carriages are everywhere—lined up at the station terminal and all along the street. Some are fashionable and sleek, pulled by a team of horses, while others are led by only one horse driven by men perched on high seats. Gentlemen in top hats escort ladies in hoop skirts along the broad sidewalks. Mother straightens her shoulders and looks from left to right, as if searching.

"Mother?" I ask.

I am interrupted by the clip clop of hooves on cobble stones. A stately coach comes to a stop before us. Two fine black horses stamp and snort. The carriage is deep red and highly polished. An open driver's seat is positioned in the front, and in the back, a hood to protect travelers from poor weather. My mouth opens in astonishment. I look to Mother. *We cannot afford a hired coach.*

"It was sent by Balthazar," she explains with a smile. "He told me to look for his crest painted upon his carriage."

Crest? Only the truly wealthy and the gentry bear such signs. I look to the carriage again. Burnished into the gleaming red door is a white raven's head surrounded by a wreath of golden leaves. The black-booted driver takes the reins in hand and, after doing some sort of fancy knot tying, steps out and stands at attention. He doesn't speak, but takes off his cap and nods, then helps us into the coach.

Once inside, I am amazed by the comfort. The seats are black studded leather and highly padded. There is room for only the two of us, but each side has a large window, plus the one in the front, through which we can see our driver. This Balthazar must certainly be wealthy, I imagine, to afford such a luxury. With a flick of the coachman's reins, we are off. Crowds of pedestrians mob the streets. There is so much to see, I can barely take it in.

We are on a street called the Strand, which winds its way along the River Thames. I am dazzled by the large buildings and the sights. "This is Charing Cross," Mother points out, "in the city of Westminster. This will lead us to the West End, where we will meet Balthazar."

My eyes are drawn to a large open space. A towering column soars skyward, and two fountains shimmer with water. "Trafalgar Square," Mother says.

The name is familiar, and I recall a lesson from my governess. "Nelson's Column," I say proudly. "After Admiral Lord Nelson, who defeated the French at the Battle of Trafalgar."

"That's correct, Jess."

She called me Jess. Mother hardly ever uses my pet name.

For a moment I forget our mission, and marvel at the sights before me. Throughout the square, there are several plinths on which stand statues of men in all their military finery: on horseback, brandishing swords, their faces peering out onto the London streets. There is one magnificient building with giant columns in the front and a dome on top. "The National Gallery," Mother says. "Father and I often—"

She stops short.

"Mother?"

She sniffles and feigns a smile, then clasps my hand. I feel a deep sorrow for the loss she has suffered.

Soon, we arrive on a grand street with fashionable shops and large townhouses. The driver slows, and we turn onto a lane off the main road. Set farther back from the street, a large house looms behind a closed gate. Two men are on either side as if standing sentry. To my surprise, they draw open the massive gate and let us pass. *Surely this can't be where Balthazar lives.* The house looks fit for royalty. I look to Mother for a moment, but she is quiet. The carriage slowly makes its way up a long drive of brick squares, leading to a house that is truly a wonder to behold. The lawn is manicured to neat perfection, with several topiaries trimmed and clipped into elaborate shapes—spirals and winding ribbons; stars and a crescent moon. Stone sculptures stand on the grounds, one of them a female form covered in ivy. Tall chimneys spew streams of wood smoke, which I can smell from within the closed coach. Small turrets and brick towers reach for the sky, and diamond-paned windows sparkle in the late-after-noon light. *How can one possibly afford such an estate?* Now I am really curious to know what this Balthazar is about.

The horses whinny and snort. Several black-booted men are standing at attention. *He has footmen?* They approach the carriage and open the doors, then take our bags and lead us into the house. Another man, one whose face looks carved from granite, nods politely. "Welcome to SummerHall," he greets us. "Please. Follow me if you will." And with a sweep of his arm, he turns and leads the way inside.

SummerHall, I muse. *How lovely.* But then it dawns on me again why we are here.

Ashes! Ashes! We all fall down!

Inside, Mother shoots me a glance. I can't fully read her expression, but it seems to be one of anxiety paired with curiosity. I try my best to keep my mouth from gaping as I take in the hall. Two giant marble columns stand at either end. I raise my head to look up. Several chandeliers glitter from a ceiling painted with so many colors and patterns that my head spins. All the objects here look as if they belong in a museum. Ornate paintings hang in gilded frames, busts and small statues sit on pedestals. Persian carpets lie underfoot. I could spend an eternity just looking at the things in the hall, but we come to a stop before a set of closed double doors. The butler pushes them inward without so much as a knock. "Mrs. Cora and Miss Jessamine Grace, my lord," he announces.

I swallow hard and look to Mother. *This man, Balthazar, is a lord? Why didn't she tell me?*

Strangely, she doesn't seem impressed at all—as if meeting aristocracy is something she does at tea every day.

I've never been "presented" before and feel a little embarrassed, but quickly put on my best ladylike charm, a trait I learned from Mother. The room we step into is absolutely spectacular. A fireplace carved from a fine, dark wood is the centerpiece, made all the more impressive by a border of intricate gold-leaf trim. Several tall candelabra are placed in each corner. Everywhere I glance, there is something of interest: a globe resting on a marble pedestal, a round clawfoot table with a display of red and white flowers, and a medieval suit of armor, silently standing sentry. Most curious of all is a large painting above the hearth of a woman in a sheer gown, running through a forest. Her hair is a lustrous black and gleams in the dark swirls of paint.

"Her name was Lady Estella," a voice rings out, and a man steps forward.

He is tall—indeed taller than any man I have seen before—and elegantly dressed. His black waistcoat is finely embroidered in a pattern of dark leaves, with silver buttons of the same motif. White lace peeks from his cuffs; his boots, which are quite fashionable, shine a deep oxblood color. Surely this must be Balthazar, and although I have never met a lord before, he is not what I would have assumed. He seems more dashing than a lord, who I always imagined would be pompous and overbearing and in possession of several chins.

He holds my gaze as I turn from the painting. "She was a faerie maiden," he says, "who was in love with a mortal man. But that is a story for another time."

He walks toward us with long steps, and I am reminded of a crane wading through tall reeds. The butler closes the double doors behind us.

Balthazar takes Mother's gloved hand in his and gently lowers his head to kiss it. "Cora, how good it is to see you again." His voice is as rich as the Devonshire cream I had at breakfast.

Mother smiles politely. "Always a pleasure," she says.

Balthazar's eyes rest a bit too long on her. She quickly turns to me. "My daughter, Jessamine Grace."

I place my left heel behind my right and dip my knees in a small curtsy, even though I am not sure if it is proper. The rules, manners, and formalities in English society are a menace to behold.

Balthazar takes my hand also—the first time a gentleman has ever done so—and lowers his head to kiss it. I do not think it is appropriate, if I recall my etiquette, but to protest would be impolite. His fingers are long and almost feminine.

"'Tis often said that the loveliest of petals bloom from the rarest of flowers," he says.

As I try to work out whether this is a compliment, I feel a wave of crimson rising up my neck.

At dinner, several footmen help us with our seats, and Balthazar takes his place at the head of the table. A man in a double-breasted black waistcoat stands at attention behind him and a little off to the side. He hasn't blinked once. Mother and I sit opposite each other.

The footmen serve small dishes from the sideboard. My stomach rumbles from the long ride, and I eat slowly, remembering my manners from *The Young Ladies' Book of Etiquette*. The heavy wood table looks fit for a party. Two candelabra with long, burning tapers are placed at either end. The china plates have an unusual pattern—the same one that was on the coach: a white raven's head circled by golden leaves.

The food is wonderful: apple and celery salad, cucumber sandwiches, boiled eggs, and, much to my horror, oysters. I've never eaten one before and am somewhat revolted by its shimmery wetness, but when I swallow, I am surprised by its taste: sharp and salty, like the sea itself. A lovely yellow custard comes last and gives a slight crackle when I tap my spoon on its surface.

Balthazar surely must know why we are really here, yet

he keeps the conversation light and full of pleasantries. His movements are so graceful—even the way he holds his knife and fork is elegant—that I feel like a complete savage.

Mother makes no mention of our reason for visiting, but nods and smiles at what seem to be the right moments.

Finally, after the staff clears away the plates, Balthazar escorts us to the library. I look to Mother. It is usually men who retire to the library after dinner, but we follow our host's lead. Heavy red draperies cover the tall windows, and a fire burns in the hearth here as well. The man must have one in every room.

Several instruments are on display, the most prominent being a piano, which is polished to perfection. I am tempted to reach out and finger the keys, although my few lessons would not be enough to attempt a tune. There is also a golden harp, three flutes of varying lengths, and a little drum. Balthazar invites us to make ourselves comfortable. After we are seated, the butler enters with drinks. "M'lady?" he offers. One hand is behind his back, and the other proffers the tray.

"A *digestif*," Balthazar explains. "A sweet lemon cordial."

I smile politely and take the small silver glass. Mother takes one as well, but Balthazar does not.

After the butler closes the door behind him, I raise the glass to my lips. The liquid is sweet and tart and reminds me of something I've tasted before but cannot place.

Balthazar sits in a heavy high-backed chair padded in

red leather. He steeples his long fingers together and looks at both of us. He wears several rings, one of which glows blood-red in the firelight. "I received your cable," he says, eyeing Mother, "and it does indeed seem to be dire news."

Finally, we're getting somewhere.

He crosses his long legs and turns to me. "Miss Jessamine," he begins. "This . . . message. Please, tell me what it said."

I know the words by heart, and feel as if I've had them in my head for years, waiting to be spoken again. "'Ring around the rosy, a pocketful of posies. Ashes! Ashes! We all fall down!'"

"*Signed*," Mother adds, "with the letter *M*."

Silence falls among us.

"So it is true," Balthazar declares softly.

"Yes," Mother answers.

There is something happening here, I realize, but at the moment I am a clueless bystander.

"And when you were in the wardrobe," he continues, "did you hear any voices? A cold breeze? A sense of . . . dread, perhaps?"

Apprehension stirs within me at the mention of dread, as if the word itself has settled on my shoulder. "No," I answer. "Nothing untoward at all."

"And the slate was in your possession the whole while?"

"Yes." I look to Mother briefly. "I entered the wardrobe

with the blank slate and replaced it with one in a hidden panel."

I feel like an absolute fraud, which is what I am, after all.

Mother shifts in her seat. "Balthazar," she begins, "you do know that my daughter and I operate, shall we say, on suggestion and desire? We do not really work in the realm of spiritualism. In common parlance, it is all a sham."

Balthazar raises an arched eyebrow. "How absolutely criminal."

Mother's lips tighten in embarrassment.

"What does it mean?" I ask. "The rhyme?"

"That, I do not know," Balthazar replies, "for I have never heard such a refrain before."

Wonderful. We came all this way, and he hasn't any answers.

Balthazar unfolds himself and stands up. I am shocked again at how very tall he is. It seems almost unnatural. "I would like to try an experiment," he suggests. "Please, gather round."

Mother and I rise and follow him to the far corner of the room, where a small circular table sits surrounded by three bentwood chairs. Mother and I sit opposite each other. Balthazar, still standing, reaches down to the edge of the table and pulls the brass knob of a drawer, which slides open with a creak. I look on curiously.

He takes out several items and places them on the table:

a sheet of cream-colored parchment, a quill and inkwell, and a leather case. After a lingering gaze at both of us—for dramatic effect only, it seems—he clicks open the hinges of the case and draws something out.

"A spirit board," I whisper. Mother and I have used these before, but never one so fine. It seems to be made of rosewood. The sun and moon are at the top left and right, and the alphabet is stamped below in burnished gold.

"Indeed," Balthazar confirms. "One that has many uses." He withdraws another object from the case. It is a planchette, a heart-shaped piece of wood used with a spirit board to receive messages from the other side.

Mother eyes the table. "Balthazar," she starts. "I told you we do not really—"

"Please," he interrupts. "Indulge me, Cora. Just for a moment." He smiles, showing perfect white teeth. It's odd to hear a gentleman address Mother with such familiarity.

Mother lets out a small sigh, and Balthazar finally sits, facing the both of us. He nudges the planchette toward me with two fingers.

Why is he giving this to me?

He reaches for the quill and dips it into the inkwell. He then begins to write on the parchment, and his forehead wrinkles in concentration. Try as I might, I cannot read the words, for they are as small and as cramped as bird tracks. The only sound is the quill tip rasping on paper. After a moment he purses his lips and blows on the wet ink, then folds the parchment lengthwise and slides it toward Mother.

"Miss Jessamine," he begins, turning to me, "if you would be so kind as to look at me and concentrate. Place your fingers on the planchette."

I take a breath and place my fingertips lightly on the polished wood object. The room is growing a little too warm for my comfort, and I wish more than anything to relieve myself of petticoats.

"Now," he says, "I want you to think of what I just wrote on that parchment. Let your thoughts drift and focus on mine."

I exhale and hope that the dampness I feel on my face is not showing. Mother has always said it is unseemly for a lady to sweat.

I stare at Balthazar, feeling a little taken aback. I've done this before with our clients, but knowing it was all a ruse made it easier, something that helped me play the part. This is entirely different. *Am I supposed to look into his mind?*

I will myself not to look away—although I am quite embarrassed, for we are sitting rather close to each other—and continue to gaze into his eyes. I focus on his thoughts, just as he has asked. I don't really know what I am doing, but I concentrate on his face. Suddenly my fingertips tingle, and the planchette seems to move of its own accord. To the left, now right, now left again. There is a pause in the tingling, but just as suddenly, I feel it again, running up and down my arms. I try to stay focused and, resisting the urge to look down, continue to stare at Balthazar. My heart races. My pulse quickens. My hands float around the board, accompanied by the scrape of the planchette. Mother's breathing sounds as loud as a trumpeting elephant. Balthazar watches with an expression of fascination.

And then I see it.

Above Balthazar's head, a thin stream of black smoke swirls in lazy circles. I gasp.

"What is it?" Mother whispers.

But I don't answer. I only gaze at the wisp of smoke that is now growing longer and climbing toward the ceiling. Balthazar leans forward slightly, his face intense in the firelight. "Do you see it?" he asks. His voice is not as calm as before, but urgent, serious.

"I do," I say, as if in a trance. Now the smoke floats back down and slithers along the table. It is thick and dark, so much so that it looks like a black mirror, completely blotting out the spirit board. Thin tendrils break off from the larger mass like long fingers, curling and twisting, taking on some sort of shape.

"Jessamine," Mother says again, following my eyes, "what do you see?"

"Letters," I say. "I see words."

"Which words?" asks Balthazar.

I stare at the smoke, which is still swirling but growing thinner, breaking apart like clouds clearing to blue skies. "Rose," I say quickly. "Dawn. Aurora."

And just like that, as if it were a figment of my imagination, the smoke vanishes.

I exhale a labored breath. My arms are sore, and white spots swim in my vision. Balthazar smiles weakly and looks to Mother, who unfolds the parchment. She is silent for a moment, and then her eyes widen. "The same words you see here," she says. "*And* the ones you spelled out with the planchette."

I stare at the words written in Balthazar's small, elegant script. "How?" I whisper.

Balthazar's eyes flash. "It can mean only one thing," he says.

"What?" I ask, growing impatient. "What does it mean?"

"You, Miss Jessamine," he says, "are a mesmerist."

CHAPTER FOUR

The Most Peculiar
of Evenings

For a moment, no one speaks. "What is a mesmerist?" I finally ask.

"A mesmerist has prophetic dreams and can read the thoughts of others," Balthazar replies. "They can make shadows appear where none exist, and cast illusions that break one's spirit."

I look into the glowing embers of the fire.

"With proper guidance," he continues, "they can force others to do their bidding, putting them under their complete power." He points this out calmly, as if offering me more tea. "Some say they can even talk to the dead."

I feel as if my senses have left me. *Talk to the dead?*

Mother seems to have lost the power of speech again, just as she had with Dr. Barnes.

"What is it?" I ask, trying my best to gather myself. "What is the smoke?"

"It is thought made material," Balthazar answers, "something that surrounds every one of us, but only a rare few can see it. Those like you, Miss Jessamine."

Those like me.

"You read the words in my mind, and also made them appear," he finishes.

Mother's face is ashen. "How?" she finally asks, looking at neither Balthazar nor me.

"She is coming into her power," Balthazar replies.

At this point I am completely flabbergasted. "What power? Where did I get it? Mother, what is this all about?"

Silence.

Mother folds her hands in her lap. "Jessamine—" she begins. "There is something I must tell you. It may come as a shock, and for that, I truly ask your forgiveness."

I wonder what can be more shocking than learning that I have a special power.

"Your father . . . " she says. "He was more than just a barrister. You see, he had an ability, if you will. The same one you now seem to possess."

"Alexander Grace was one of our strongest members," Balthazar adds. "It is a great loss that we no longer have him on our side."

On our side?

Mother inhales sharply, and her response is met by an inquisitive gaze from Balthazar. "Cora. You have told Jessamine nothing?"

Mother shakes her head. "I was prepared to do so. Soon."

Now I am utterly confused.

Balthazar steeples his fingers together again and nods, as if thinking.

"What do you mean?" I demand. "Told me what?"

"Jess," Mother says—*she called me Jess again*—"your father, Balthazar, and I once belonged to an order."

I pause. "Order?"

"We were known as the League of Ravens," Balthazar says, his voice echoing about the room. "For it is the raven that is the protector of Britain, from days of old."

"There are supernatural forces in the world, Jessamine," Mother adds. "Our order kept the world—or at least England —safe from such threats."

I open my mouth but words fail me. I need time to breathe and sort this all out. It seems as if an eternity passes. "What is it?" I finally ask. "The *M*. What does it stand for?"

"The *M* is the mark of Mephisto," Balthazar says. "Once

the greatest threat London had ever known. A malevolent order that lived in darkness and fed on fear. They are necromancers, Miss Jessamine."

"Necromancers?" I question. The word is unfamiliar on my tongue.

"Those who summon the dead," Mother says flatly.

I swallow hard.

"They were destroyed years ago," Balthazar says, "but when they killed your father—"

"What?" I cry out as a sharp pain jolts through me. "Mother. What is this? Father died of consumption."

"No, Jessamine. Your father killed one of these creatures, but in doing so, he suffered grievous wounds."

Balthazar lowers his head for a moment and then raises it. His expression is grim. "There was nothing we could do to save him. And now, as I have feared, it seems they are back."

I stare into the fire. My mind is blank, emotionless. I feel as if I am sinking into a black hole. The emptiness suddenly turns to anger. I realize that my right hand is tightly clenched into a fist. "Mother—" I almost hiss. "How could you? *All this time?* To not have told me the truth?"

She flushes. "And what would you have me say, Jessamine? That your dear papa was killed by a monster? That his body was rip—" She closes her mouth in midsentence. Her eyes are damp. Red splotches rise up her neck.

Balthazar tries to ease the tension that is now hanging like a shroud. "It was eight years ago, Miss Jessamine, when you were but a child of five. She did what she had to do to protect you."

I feel like screaming.

Mother takes out a silk cloth and wipes her eyes. A heavy silence fills the room. And then it hits me. "Wait—" I glance at Mother. "If you and Papa were members of this order, then you must have an ability too."

"I once had a gift," she says wearily. "But now, try as I might, it seems to have left me."

"Tell me," I demand, not caring if I sound cross. "What was it?"

She closes her eyes and exhales. Balthazar cocks his head, like a curious bird. I stare at Mother for what surely must be several minutes. Suddenly her face *ripples*. There is something else there, something under the surface, wavering back and forth. Her hair, which is dark and lustrous, is now flickering with a reddish hue. Freckles bloom on her delicate pale skin. Her nose, sharp and aquiline, has become small and upturned. Releasing a labored breath, she opens her eyes. The illusion fades in front of me, and she is back to the mother I know.

"At one time," she tells me, "I was an illusionist. I could change my appearance so others would see someone else."

"Unbelievable," I murmur quietly, suddenly accepting

the whole bizarre affair. Mother slumps in her chair a little, as if exhausted.

Balthazar stirs in his seat. "I have discovered that those who manifest these abilities do so while young. Something about the innocence of youth heightens their powers. In time, as we grow older, they seem to fade."

"And what of you?" I ask, coming back to myself, fixing my gaze on him. "Do you have a special power?" I'm afraid of what will be revealed next on this, the most peculiar of evenings.

A sardonic smile forms on his face. After a breath, his voice lifts and he speaks, but as I listen, it is more like a melody, and it seems as if the instruments in the room are accompanying him.

> "Long ago, in the early days of the world,
> When man still walked among the ancient groves,
> And every doorstep led to a lush green meadow,
> Men and women often visited the Twilight Folk,
> And with leaves in their hair, danced in dizzying circles
> To the trill of the flute and the beat of the drum,
> To fall into a deep reverie under a thousand twinkling stars,
> Only to awake to find themselves entwined in an embrace,
> Fae and mortal bound together."

I open my eyes, which I didn't know were closed, and shake

my head, as if awakening from a dream. Embers pop and hiss in the fireplace. "And that would mean what?" I ask, a little too sharply.

"I am of the gentry," he says.

"I took you for the sort," I say. This feels a little petty, but all attempts at propriety have escaped me.

"We are also called the Traveling Folk."

I stare, dumbfounded.

"Most commonly," he continues, "we are called faeries."

"Faeries," I say. It is not a question. I glance at Mother. Surely this man is mad, but she gives no sign that is the case.

"Truth be told," Balthazar explains, "in my case, I am only half fae. The blood of the folk runs through my veins, as does that of the mortal race."

It is then that I wish I were old enough for a drink.

"Jessamine," Mother says, "I know this must seem unbelievable, to say the least."

I stare at Balthazar.

Faeries. He said he was a faerie.

A servant comes in and quietly stokes the fire. I am beyond weary, yet my thoughts are racing—the trip, this fantastical story, Papa—I don't even know where to begin. I turn to Mother. I can't let it go. A lump grows in my throat. "Why didn't you ever tell me?" I ask. "About yourself, and Papa?"

"I thought the work of the order was behind us," she replies. "I thought we could go on to live our lives without the horror of the past. I wanted to protect you, Jessamine."

I can see the grief on her face, etched in small lines around her mouth and eyes.

Balthazar glances at the spirit board. "But now we receive this message from Mephisto at the same time you are revealed to be a mesmerist. Coincidence? I think not."

"They have come out of the darkness." Mother says. "But who is leading them, and why?"

Balthazar's long face is troubled. For the first time, I see tiny wrinkles at the corners of his eyes. "As of late, throughout the East End, there have been reports of graveyards being desecrated, and of a creeping shadow at night, one that leaves only a trail of crimson blood."

My stomach turns.

"Whatever they seek," he continues, and his eyes sweep over mine to land on Mother, "I believe they will surely come after those closest to Alexander."

Fear grips my heart. "What do you mean?" I demand, looking at him and then at her. "Us? Me?"

"Your father and I were instrumental in stopping Mephisto in the past," Mother says. "They will surely seek retribution."

The word "retribution" hangs in the air like a thundercloud. This is all too terrible to bear. I feel as if I will faint. My head spins. *It's all a dream,* I suddenly realize. Any moment now I'll wake up and find myself on the floor in our parlor. It was the fall I took from the cabinet. I'm unconscious; that's it. All of this—the trip to London, Balthazar, talk of faeries and a secret order—it's all in my head.

"And that is why we need you, Miss Jessamine," Balthazar finishes, bringing me back to the room. "To stay strong and fight this threat."

I stare at my boots.

"But not tonight," Mother objects, coming to my aid. "We are tired, and Jessamine has just received news that would unsettle the hardiest of souls."

Balthazar rises from his chair. "Please forgive me. I sometimes forget the human need for sleep, something my kind does not require."

Unbelievable.

"The hour is late," he adds. "I should have realized. Get some rest. Both of you. Tomorrow will be brighter."

I look to Mother, then to Balthazar.

After this evening's news, I am not so certain of that.

I am too flummoxed to try to sleep. *A secret order? Talk of evil men and summoners of the dead? And me? A mesmerist? How can this be?*

Under any other circumstances I would be impressed by the guest room, but my mind is muddled from the day's events. There is a beautiful hand-painted silk screen to dress behind, an armoire carved from burnished wood, finely wrought tables and chairs, and on the vanity, a lovely music box encrusted with jewels. The four-poster bed is draped with a flowing white fabric. Mother is in the room next to mine. I almost feel like knocking on her door and asking more questions, but I do not.

I sit down on the bed.

A light knock startles me. "Come in," I call, and stand up.

The door creaks open, and a young servant enters. She seems to be of an age with me, perhaps a year younger. She is rather plain looking, I must admit, with drab brown hair that falls to her shoulders. She has the look of a country girl about her. I can picture her milking a cow. I scold myself for my assumptions.

She sets down a tray of hot milk and biscuits, keeping her head lowered the whole time. I have forgotten how docile servants can be, now that we no longer have any.

"Thank you," I say, and try to catch her eye, but her gaze remains downcast. Like most servants, I would assume, she daren't speak to her master's guests. "What is your name?" I ask, although I don't know why. Perhaps for a bit of normalcy on this unbelievable evening.

The girl gives an awkward curtsy. "Darby, miss."

"I'm Jess," I offer.

She curtsies again, her eyes to the floor.

"Darby is a lovely name," I tell her. "And how long have you been in service?"

She slowly raises her head.

I almost gasp.

One side of her face is horribly burned. Cold white scars run down her cheek and onto her neck. My first instinct is to recoil, but I catch myself before that happens.

"I have worked for m'lord going on five years now, miss."

"And is he a kind master?" I ask. I wonder how much she knows about this League of Ravens business.

"Yes, miss. Very kind indeed. If it weren't for him, I'd be . . ." She trails off, a look of alarm on her face.

I have tormented her enough, I realize. Whatever her story is, it must be painful.

"Well, it was a pleasure to meet you, Darby," I say cheerily, although it belies the tension that hangs silently in the room.

But Darby doesn't answer, only dips her head and scurries out.

When sleep finally comes, I sink into a murky world of shadows. There is a tunnel before me, with bright light in the distance. The ground rumbles. White fog surrounds me. My heart is pounding. Something is coming, but I do not know what, and only feel its presence, a terrible shadow that slithers along the ground, leaving a trail of crimson blood in its wake.

CHAPTER FIVE

The Sleeping Man

I awake to servants chattering in the hall.

The strangeness of last evening comes back to me. It wasn't a dream after all: talk of faeries and a secret order, Mother's face rippling in the firelight, Father killed by a creature of the dark, *his body rip—*

I close my eyes. "Dear Papa," I whisper.

Of all the unbelievable revelations, this disturbs me most. Father was a gentle soul, and even though I was only five when he died, I do remember him fondly: his long, somber face, his eyes, so gray they looked almost silver. One memory remains vivid, in contrast to the little I recall from my early years here in London. It is of Father and I walking in the botanical gardens, his hands clasped behind his back, his strides so long I had to gather my skirts to keep up. Just thinking of it now makes me sniffle. As we walked, he would point out flowering shrubs and plants with a nod of his head. "There lies *Aspidistra*," he'd say. Or "Behold, the lovely summer snowflake, almost as beautiful as you, my dear child."

And then he would lift his voice and sing:

"The smile upon her bonnie cheek
Was sweeter than the bee;
Her voice excelled the birdie's song
Upon the birchen tree."

The memory brings a feeling of melancholia that cuts deep. I feel a tingle behind my eyes, and before I can stop myself, tears are on my cheeks.

Breakfast is served in the same dining hall as dinner the night before. The day is pleasant, with sunlight streaming through the windows and birds chirping outside. Mother's eyes are red, as if she didn't sleep at all.

The table holds a bounty of foods, certainly more than enough for the three of us: black pudding, baked breads, mushrooms, beans, back bacon, scones, omelets, and several jars of jam and marmalade. Balthazar picks at a melon of some sort with ruby-red skin. Small seeds are revealed in the pulpy white membrane. "A pomegranate," he offers as he catches my stare. "A very ancient food. Would you care to partake?"

I politely decline, although I am curious, as I have never seen such an odd fruit before.

Mother sips her tea. All she has on her plate is buttered toast, so I follow her lead, although I add marmalade to mine.

There is something I want to ask, and after yesterday, I feel that nothing is out of bounds. "The servant—" I start. "Darby. What happened to her?"

Mother gives me a look as if I am being impolite, but I return her stare. Darby's affairs are none of my concern, but I need to know more about the cold white scars.

"The tale of Darby is a strange one," Balthazar begins.

I wonder about that. *Stranger than meeting a man who says he is a faerie? And that I am a mesmerist?*

Balthazar crosses his long legs. "A few years back, my travels took me to the glorious city of Rome, where, every day, I took long, leisurely walks. Upon one of these afternoons, I found myself wandering beyond the city streets to a small village in the mountains." He pauses and sips his tea. Mother now decides to spread marmalade on her toast, and for some reason, the scrape of the knife sets my nerves on edge.

"I heard a ruckus—screams and cries in the air. Black clouds of smoke rose from the town square. I made my way there and found, to my horror, a ghastly scene."

"What was it?" I ask, almost not wanting to know. *What could possibly frighten a man who has seen necromancers?*

"A young girl, lashed to a cross, with flames roaring around her. I saw the terror on her face. It was barbaric." His brow furrows. "The priest had condemned her as a lycanthrope."

I give him a questioning look.

"A werewolf," he says calmly.

"Werewolf," I whisper, bringing to mind something out of a penny dreadful, one of those beastly stories told in pulpy newspapers.

"Several children in the town had gone missing, you see, and the villagers claimed it was the work of werewolves."

I swallow hard.

"I learned that the girl's parents had suffered the same fate that was about to befall her. I had no choice but to convince the priest to let me take her into my care."

It can't be, I tell myself. "Darby?"

"Yes," Balthazar replies.

I gasp, and look from him to Mother—for anything that will convince me this isn't true, but her face is stoic. "But surely they were wrong, weren't they? She isn't really a . . ." I can't bring myself to say the word again.

"Werewolf?" Balthazar suggests.

I nod meekly.

"Yes," he says. "I'm afraid so."

I close my eyes and open them again. I stare at the bright white tablecloth.

"She is an orphan," Balthazar explains. "And I have treated her affliction as well as I am able. The first few years were less than desirable, but now she willingly takes a potion to keep the disease at bay."

An image of Darby being burned alive rises in front of my vision. It is too much to bear, and I shut it out of my mind.

Will the strangeness of this trip never end?

Balthazar dabs his napkin at the corner of his mouth. "We must depart," he declares. "There are people you should both meet, and time is of the essence."

"What?" I ask. "Where?"

"Someplace *entirely* different from SummerHall," he slyly hints.

"But we have to return home," I protest. "We didn't pack for another trip."

"I'm sorry to inconvenience you, Miss Jessamine. It is not a great distance, but it is a trip of the utmost importance. I must alert my colleagues to the news you have brought."

I turn to Mother. I am not sure I want to be involved in any of this. But she does not come to my aid. "Let us see this out, Jessamine," she says, "and then you can decide upon what you wish to do."

I sigh.

What I want to do, I now realize, is return home and put this awful business behind me.

Mother comes into my guest room as we prepare to leave. "What is happening?" I round on her. "We came here for answers, and now we are being taken elsewhere. I don't even have proper shoes!"

She clasps my hands. I look into her eyes, which are light green and stand out against her fair skin. "There are many things in this world we cannot control, Jessamine. But we do have choices, and I will support yours, whatever they may be. I promise you."

And then she kisses me on the cheek. I am surprised at this, as it is something she seldom does, although we love each other dearly. The comforting scent of Cameo Rose puts me at ease. "I know it has been difficult, Jess," she consoles me, "learning all this so quickly."

Jess.

"Your father . . . I am sorry I was not able to tell you the truth. It was all done to protect you, my dear."

"How did he die?" I ask. The question comes quickly, before I even think to ask it.

Mother blinks several times. "Perhaps we should wait on that story, Jessamine."

Jessamine. She's all business again. "Mother—"

But we are interrupted by one of Balthazar's footmen, who arrives to tell us it is time to depart.

The sky is cloudy when we leave SummerHall. The carriage is even grander than the one that arrived for us at the station. The exterior is a lustrous black, free of blemishes or dents. At the front of the coach, two gas lamps are perched on either side to provide light for night driving. The same crest is emblazoned on the doors: a white raven's head surrounded by a golden wreath. *Is this a faerie emblem?* I wonder now. I am struck again by the oddness of it all.

The driver pulls a lever, and a set of small steps extend to the ground so we do not have to exert ourselves as we enter the coach. The fabric of the seats is deep blue, bordered with paisley swirls. Fringes and little tassels hang from the doors. There are even foot warmers and pillows. For a moment, the luxury of the coach eases my frustration. I sit beside Mother, and Balthazar takes a seat opposite us.

The ride is comfortable, for the road is laid with tracks. We pass more stately homes, and I look out the window in fascination. On the northeast corner, past Trafalgar Square, a church with a towering white steeple comes into view. Stone steps lead up to massive columns. Balthazar notices my curiosity. "St. Martin-in-the-Fields," he points out. "Once, there were many fields around this area, hence the name."

"It's beautiful," I murmur.

"The human need for penance is strong," he replies wistfully. "I find it fascinating, this devotion."

Just as I am about to ask him to explain further, the driver slows and we come to a stop. I look around. The buildings and shops are familiar. "This is Charing Cross," I say, perplexed.

"Why are we stopped?" Mother asks, peering out the window.

"I am afraid my landau would look quite out of place where we are going," Balthazar replies. "We will have to travel by bus from here."

"Bus?" I question. I am ashamed to admit I am enjoying the luxury of the coach.

No one replies, but the driver extends the steps so we can exit. Mother gives me a small smile, as if to say she is sorry for all that is being put upon me.

I do not smile back.

The "bus," as Balthazar called it, is an omnibus, and looks to be a horrid means of transport. It is a large coach pulled by three draft horses. Several people are inside, sitting perilously close to one another—some read newspapers; others seem to be asleep. There is a woman clutching her bag tightly to her chest, a man who looks as if he has a very close relationship with gin, and several others who smell as if they could use a bath.

I am shocked to see that the floor is covered with musty straw. Balthazar shoots Mother and me a sympathetic look. A man coughs, and I hold my handkerchief demurely to my nose. I surely would have preferred Balthazar's landau. I wonder why he cannot simply snap his fingers and have us transported there. After all, he says he is a faerie. *Exactly what can a faerie do?*

Although there is a chill in the air outside, the cabin is so hot and stuffy, I feel faint. Once again, I sit beside Mother, and Balthazar sits opposite us. Hopefully, the trip will not take too long.

There are people you should both meet.

What people? I wonder.

I awake, startled.

The man across the aisle from me is snoring loudly, and his whiskered mustache blows out with each creaky whistle. I didn't even realize I had dozed off. I sit up and compose myself. *How horrid,* I think, *falling asleep in this dreadful carriage.* Most unladylike.

53

The man continues to snore like a bellows. He is a very large fellow, and I expect the buttons on his vest to burst at any moment and scatter in the aisle.

I look briefly to Mother, who gazes out the window with a distant air about her. Balthazar pores over a book, his head down. I turn to the man again.

Can I see what he is thinking?

I block out the hot cabin, the sharp odor of someone's greasy chips, the clatter of the horses' hooves, and focus all my energy on a spot on the man's cheek, a red blemish resembling a cluster of grapes. After a moment I feel a tingle in the center of my head.

And then it happens again.

A ribbon of rusty red smoke trails from his forehead and across the aisle. I look left, then right. No one notices. *How can they not see it?*

I wave my hand in the air and feel the mist curl around my fingers, but I lower it when I see Balthazar shoot me a glance. I return my gaze to the sleeping man. The tendrils swirl around his head. There are no smoky words this time, but I feel a jolt, like pins and needles on the back of my neck. A series of images flashes before my eyes: a small room filled with rubbish, a red-faced, squalling child, and a woman, drying her tears with a frayed handkerchief.

"Morris," the woman pleads. *"She is your child. Your daughter!"*

"The child is not mine!" a man's voice cries out. *"Put the bastard in an orphanage!"*

The man snorts and opens his eyes.

He is staring right at me.

I squeeze the armrest of my seat. *I'm done for. He knows.* But much to my relief, he snuffles once, closes his eyes, and immediately begins snoring again.

A sharp pain stabs my temples. For a moment I am dizzy and feel quite tired. I close my eyes. When I open them again, Balthazar is staring at me.

I saw the man's memories in my mind's eye. How is that possible?

It is an invasion of sorts, I realize, this gift of mine—eavesdropping to the highest degree. Father had this ability. *How did he use it? How did he die?* The questions seem to never end.

The wealth and luxury of the West End is a thing of the past now as the bus pulls into a warren of crooked streets. It's darker here, although the sun is peeking through scattered gray clouds. A yellow fog hangs over everything. "Welcome to the East End," Balthazar says glumly.

This neighborhood is cramped with small houses crowded together. People are everywhere: standing in front of their doors, sitting on buckets, sweeping up dusty steps. A foul odor rises on the air. I wrinkle my nose.

"The Thames," Mother says. I look to the window. Several men and boys are gathered at the banks of the river. They look a sorry lot, with trouser legs rolled up to reveal knobby knees as pale as fish bellies. "This is the same river we saw from the West End," I observe. "But it smells worse here."

"I am fortunate enough to reside *upwind* of the river," Balthazar says.

"Who are they?" I ask. "The men down there."

"Mudlarks," he replies. "They scavenge the murky depths for things they can sell: scraps of metal, bits of iron, broken pieces of wood and coal."

How awful, I think, *to have to resort to such unseemly work.*

The omnibus comes to a stop, and Balthazar helps us both out. "Follow me, if you will. It's not too far now."

I wonder what "it" is.

I share a glance with Mother. "Exactly where are you taking us?" she demands.

Balthazar pauses. "I would not lead you astray, Cora. Please, we are expected."

And then he's off again. Mother and I have no choice but to follow.

Balthazar takes long strides, which reminds me of Father, and I walk quickly to keep pace with him. I thought a gentleman should walk in unison with a lady, offering his arm if need be. So much for my fanciful thoughts.

We pass a street doctor selling vials and potions from an open leather case perched on a high table. "Sassafras," he calls in a singsong voice, "a cure-all for what ails you." Farther down the road, a man in a top hat sits on a stool, mending the seat of a cane chair. Shoeblacks shine gentlemen's shoes, and cries of "Chestnuts! Hot chestnuts!" ring in the air.

I am certainly no longer in Deal.

Up ahead, our way is blocked by some sort of disturbance. Several men are digging up the earth, as if trying to reach Hell itself. Mounds of dirt are everywhere. Steel beams are stacked like firewood. Several homes have been demolished, and the remains are roped off from passersby. Horse-drawn wagons rattle along, their beds heaped with refuse.

"What is this?" I ask.

"They are building a new way of transport," Balthazar explains. "They call it the Underground. Steam-powered locomotives that will ferry passengers all about London."

I look at the massive holes again. Large, towering cranes creak and groan. *It's impossible,* I tell myself. *Under the earth?* "I don't imagine that will ever happen," I say.

Mother gathers her skirts and steps out of the way of a barefoot boy running amidst the wreckage. "Pies!" he calls out. "Hot pies!"

"Balthazar," she implores, annoyed. "How much farther?"

"Not too long," he promises, and we make our way around the work site. Mother brushes an errant lock of hair from her face. Her forehead is damp, and I want to tell her.

Finally Balthazar stops before a row of gloomy brick houses, all connected, each with its own little white steps. A brass plate nailed into the brick reads 17 WADSWORTH PLACE. The door we stand in front of is covered in ivy and feels ominous to me, as if my life will be changed forever if I step through.

"Are you ready?" he asks, looking to Mother and then me, a gleam in his eyes.

"Ready for what?" we both ask.

"To meet the League of Ravens," he says.

CHAPTER SIX

17 Wadsworth Place

The house smells damp. Balthazar leads us through the foyer and into a sitting room, at the center of which is a large circular table surrounded by chairs. Off to the right I see another door, which must lead to a parlor. Fringed yellow curtains cover the windows, and oil lamps provide a weak light. Books are everywhere: teetering on end tables, stacked in corners, and jumbled under a small flight of stairs. Curious objects are placed on shelves. Little ornaments and paintings adorn the walls. But what truly gives me pause is a stuffed bird in a cage, a large white raven whose dead eyes seem to follow me as I study the room.

And then I see the children.

A girl, who looks a year or two younger than I am, leans lazily against the mantel of a fireplace. White-blond hair frames an angelic face. She is so pale her skin is almost translucent, and the red dress she wears gleams in bold contrast. She looks up and smiles shyly.

Opposite her, a boy with a mop of black curls sits cross-legged on the floor, scribbling in a small book, completely oblivious to our presence. He is dressed in a suit, with brown knickers and white stockings.

"Jessamine—" Balthazar begins. "Cora—it is my pleasure to introduce you to the League of Ravens."

The boy looks up, smiles, and then returns to his book.

Mother eyes both children warily.

"The disturbing reports I spoke of have prompted me to find new recruits," Balthazar tells us. "Ones with supernatural abilities, to take up our cause."

He turns to me. "Just like you, Miss Jessamine."

I recall his words from the night before:

As of late, throughout the East End, there have been reports of graveyards being desecrated, and of a creeping shadow at night, one that leaves only a trail of crimson blood.

His face suddenly takes on a grave expression. "The dark is rising. It is time for a new generation to stop the evil that is stirring in the shadows."

Before I have a chance to fully comprehend his dire warning, the girl drifts away from the window, like a ghost. Her steps are quiet. "I'm Emily," she says brightly. "It's a pleasure to meet you." She recites this carefully, as if it has been rehearsed. Her eyes are a startling blue, so large they look almost like a doll's.

"I'm Jess," I say.

Balthazar waves a hand at the boy on the floor. "And over here is Master Gabriel."

I take a few steps closer to the boy. "Well," I say. "It is a pleasure to meet you, Gabe."

"Gabriel," he says without looking up.

I wilt, taken aback by his brusqueness.

"C'mon," Emily says. "So what are you about, then?"

"I'm sorry?" I question. Her speech has the cadence of working-class London, a dialect I'd heard from some of the men down at the docks.

"What can you do?" she clarifies.

Balthazar smiles and, in a low voice, says, "Miss Jessamine has just discovered her power, Emily. She will need a little time to—"

"No." I cut him off. "I can show her."

Balthazar smiles. Mother watches me cautiously.

Just as I did with the man on the bus, I focus on Emily's thoughts. I exhale and match my breathing with hers.

In . . . and out. In . . . and out. Emily's eyes seem to change color—icy blue one moment and emerald green the next. She stares at me as I concentrate, but I do not look away.

And then I see the smoke again.

It trails from Emily's head to mine and reminds me of glittering moss after a spring rain. I feel Mother's gaze on me.

I close my eyes, and a scene comes up behind them: *A lace curtain billows lazily from an open window, letting in the sour smell of refuse and garbage from outside. I can smell it, as if I am right there. A younger Emily is sleeping on the floor of a shabby room, wrapped in a ratty blanket. She hugs a dolly to her chest. Across from her, a man slumps in a chair, a bottle gripped in his hand. His face is worn and anxious.*

I feel myself wanting to break away—this is too private, I realize—but my eyes remain closed, as if I have no power to resist the memory that has unfolded before me.

"I'll not have it in my house," the man says. *"The girl's touched."*

He is talking to a woman with red-knuckled hands and a thin, drawn face. Tears glisten on her cheeks. *"But she's only four, Oliver,"* she says. *"A child."*

"All the easier for the devil to do his mischief," the man answers. *"I seen the fire inside her."*

"I'll see to her," the woman pleads. *"She won't be a bother. Promise."*

The scene breaks, and for a moment, with eyes still closed, I think that is all, but . . .

"No!" the woman cries. "Oliver, please!"

The man called Oliver grabs Emily's small wrist with thick, callused fingers. "Come along, girl," he snarls, tugging her away. "I won't have evil in me own house!"

"No!" Emily cries. "Mam!"

But it is too late.

He pushes her through the door and leads her screaming up the street.

Outside, the sky is iron gray. Rain begins to fall. Emily struggles against the man's fierce grip. "I want me mam!" she cries.

The man is a lumbering giant, pulling her along like a rag doll, stopping every now and then to take a swig from the brown bottle.

I see their destination up ahead.

An old brick mansion, covered in vines and sitting in the shade of thick trees like a sleeping brown beast. Black smoke puffs from a chimney. A few shattered windows dot the façade like a smile gone wrong.

The man kneels and pulls Emily close. For a moment, I think he is going to hug her to his chest, but instead, he fishes in his pockets and pulls out a torn piece of paper. He pins it to Emily's ragged dress:

CANNA CARE FOR. PLEAS TAKE. GOES BY EMILY.
GOD BLES.

I open my eyes. I feel a sharp pain along my neck and shoulders, but it passes within seconds. I feel as if I have done the most dreadful thing imaginable, looking in on someone's private world. Everyone is staring at me. "I'm sorry," I say to Emily. "I saw what you were thinking . . . when he took you away. That man. Oliver. He was your fath—"

"Ah, he were nothing but a big lummox," Emily cuts me off. "It's better now. I got a new family." She smiles, showing small teeth. "Miss me mam, though."

There is a moment of silence.

Balthazar and Gabriel both smile. Emily doesn't seem bothered that I have so quickly learned of her terrible past.

Balthazar nods like a proud headmaster. "Very good, Miss Jessamine. You are learning quickly. We will need all your strength in the fight to come."

I'm not so sure about that, I think. *I just want this all to go away.*

"And what about you?" I ask Emily, coming back to myself. "What is your ability?"

Emily glances at Balthazar. He shakes his head, very slightly.

"Plenty of time for that," he says. "Come. I have much to show you."

Mother and I follow him up the creaky steps. Gabriel and Emily remain downstairs. I am curious to know what their powers are. It dawns on me that if I continue on this path, I will learn soon enough.

Upstairs, there is a narrow hallway with doors along each side. Drab wallpaper with a pattern of roses peels from the walls. Mother takes it all in with a sour look.

"It is a safe place," Balthazar assures us, "here in Whitechapel, away from prying eyes."

"The children," Mother says all of a sudden. "How did they come to be here?"

"My sources led me to an orphanage," he replies. "Mrs. Alexandra's Home for Foundling Boys and Girls. Both children showed signs of supernatural abilities, something the Church of England believed to be the work of the devil. It was only a matter of time before they were dropped off on the stoop of the orphanage like so much baggage."

He pauses and shakes his head. *How terrible,* I think. To be abandoned by one's own mother and father.

"The headmistress was eager to see them taken in by a gentleman with an estate," he continues, "one who needed a scullery maid and a chimney sweep." He flashes a grin. "That would be me."

Mother almost rolls her eyes.

"And they look after themselves?" I ask. "Here on their own?" I find this prospect quite exciting, fending for one's self, like in one of my old stories—*The Adventures of Jess the Pirate Girl and her Deeds of Derring-Do!*—but I am not certain I could truly be on my own without Mother's love and support.

"Upon your imminent arrival," Balthazar explains, "I arranged for Emily and Gabriel to stay here for a day or two, as they are usually with me at SummerHall. I wanted to hear your news alone, first." He pauses. "But things are moving quickly. We must remain close. This will be our headquarters, so to speak."

Headquarters? I'm getting deeper in by the minute.

Balthazar opens a door to our left and we enter. This room is also cramped with old books, just as downstairs, some of them looking as if they'd crumble into dust if handled. Mother sneezes.

"The battleground of a mesmerist takes place in the mind," he says, "but members of our order must also be *physically* prepared."

I have no idea what this means.

He reaches into his waistcoat and reveals a key, then walks a few short steps to a standing wooden cabinet. We follow him and watch as he places the key into the lock on the door. It opens with a creak, and he pulls out a battered leather satchel and places it on a table. A cloud of dust rises up. "These were your father's weapons, Miss Jessamine."

Mother gasps. "I thought they were lost. I should have been told."

Balthazar nods sympathetically. "They are just here for safekeeping, Cora. I didn't want to bring up terrible memories."

She gives a slight nod in return, as if accepting his explanation. *Still,* I think, *she should have known.* It was Father's, after all.

I look at the satchel. A faded image of a raven's head is stamped into the leather. There is also a long scar, as if scored by a monstrous claw. *Was that done by the creature who killed him?*

Mother takes a few steps forward and, after what seems like a full minute, takes a breath and lifts the flap. Her expression is thoughtful and sad, and it is clear that she is thinking of Father. She pulls a black case from the satchel and opens it. Several instruments are cradled in a bed of red velvet. One of them is a braided whip, curled like a sleeping snake. The end is split into five tails. Mother draws it out. "This," she says, "is your most important weapon, Jessamine. The lash. This one has seen its fair share of battle."

Without warning, she cracks the whip. A cloud of dust flies up, revealing a ragged gash in the hardwood floor.

I stare at her. This is not the mother I know. This woman

has a fierce look in her eyes and a hard set to her jaw. Balthazar smiles. Mother seems to stand a few inches taller.

She sets the lash down and picks up another tool. "This is the compass, also very important. With it, you must bind your foe within the Circle of Confinement."

Circle of Confinement?

The compass is silver, with two shining points, and is at least twelve inches tall, larger than any compass I have ever seen, which, admittedly, was only once, in a shop window.

"When the circle is drawn," Mother explains, "a creature of the dark is bound. That is when you must drop holy water inside." She holds up a glass vial that shimmers with a clear liquid.

"And last, but most important, is a sprig from the acacia tree." She sets down the vial and lifts a small, slender branch from the case. "It has healing power, and if you ever find yourself hurt, eat one of the leaves."

"How does it stay alive?" I ask. "It's impossible." As soon as I ask the question, I know it is of no consequence, considering what I have already witnessed on this strange journey.

"The League of Ravens has always been well versed in magick and spells," Balthazar says. "The branch is enchanted with great power."

"To most people, these are just simple objects," Mother adds, "but to those with supernatural abilities, they are deadly weapons."

I look at the tools spread out on the table. *I'm expected to use these? To kill creatures, like a ruffian?*

Mother returns the tools to the case and slides it into the satchel. She folds down the flap. I run my fingers across the worn leather. "Father's weapons," I whisper, as if saying it aloud will make this all seem more real.

"They are yours now, Miss Jessamine," Balthazar says. "Use them wisely."

CHAPTER SEVEN

Departures and Decisions

Back downstairs, Emily and Gabriel have moved into what I correctly assumed was the parlor. There is a settee covered in garish pink fabric, a fireplace, several small chairs, and a table for four at which they are now seated. A deck of cards is spread out before them. They look up curiously as we enter.

"Just showing Jessamine a bit of her history," Balthazar tells them.

There is a moment of silence.

"Are we going back to SummerHall?" Emily asks.

Gabriel sets down his cards and strokes his chin,

something that looks entirely out of place for someone so young.

"I'm afraid not," Balthazar says. "We have work to do."

At Balthazar's insistence, Mother and I stay the night. My room is certainly not as comfortable as the one at Summer-Hall, but it does, at least, have a fireplace—sorely blackened and in need of cleaning. There is also a small, narrow bed, a writing desk, and a table with a basin and pitcher. In the corner is a child's chair and dresser. The window is cracked and lets in cold air that chills my neck.

Lovely, I say to myself. *Just lovely.*

I lie down on the bed. My thoughts are scattered, and I cannot seem to focus on one thing at a time. I quiet my mind enough to think back on Emily. *What would cause a father to completely abandon his child? "I seen the fire inside her," he had said. Can she transform into a dangerous animal, like Darby? And what of Gabriel?* These questions remain in my head until finally, with the wind rattling the window, I drift off to an uneasy sleep.

Tonight, I dream of a little girl.

She comes to me in a fog of swirling gray mist. Her pinafore dress is frayed and torn. Blood runs along the hem. *"Help me," she whispers. "Please. Help me."*

She reaches out a hand. Her fingers are stiff and swollen,

and when she opens her mouth again, no words come out, only a foul black liquid.

In the morning, I meet Mother in the parlor. I see no sign of breakfast and do not have an appetite anyway. She is back to her usual self, not the mysterious woman who opened Father's case and cracked his whip. *My* whip. A lash, she called it.

Fresh flowers are on the table, and the sweet smell of lavender fills the room. This gives me pause, as flowers are not in season. *Is this some sort of faerie magic?* I wonder. We sit on the settee, and she takes my hands. "My dear child," she says. "My sweet Jessamine."

Just hearing these words, I feel as if my heart will fall out. We've been through thick and thin since Father's death, and all we have is each other.

"I told you there are always choices," she begins, "and now you must decide on what yours will be."

She releases my hands. For a moment she says nothing, but looks past my head, and stares into the distance. "Your father and I were called upon to do this work too, in our younger days. We were newly married and still basking in the warm glow of first love."

I should be embarrassed by this intimate detail, but for some reason I am not. Her eyes sparkle, and I don't know if it is from the happy memory or an overwhelming feeling of loss.

"After our vows, we made our home in London," she continues, "and there, your father took up his work as a barrister. Soon after, an old friend called upon him. It was Balthazar, you see. They were at university together." She pauses and looks through a window, where the twisted branches of an elm tree cast shadows in the morning sun. She turns back to me, and her face is grave. "Balthazar told him that bodies were being found in the East End of the city. They were all missing limbs, and he needed help in discovering the cause."

I shudder. "Why would someone—"

"It was Mephisto," Mother says with a scowl, "causing havoc and chaos to some ghastly end. That incident spawned many more, and at your father's request, I joined him in the battle."

Never before have I seen Mother like this. She is always reserved, always guarded. She has kept these secrets from me for years, and now I'm beginning to understand why.

"We spent many years battling the powers of the dark, my child, and it took its toll."

She clasps my hands again, and her grip tightens, as if she is afraid she will lose me, too, just as she lost Papa. "After your father's death, I raised you in Deal, away from this dreadful city, where you could grow up near the water and the green outdoors. But now we find ourselves here once more."

She closes her eyes and releases a sigh. Everything she has done has been for me. *Everything.* I want to hug her and never let her go, but before I can, she speaks again. "And before your father died, Jess, he killed our strongest enemy, one of the greatest necromancers of all."

"Who?"

"His name was Malachai. Malachai Grimstead. Father killed him but died shortly thereafter."

"Malachai," I whisper.

"He possessed the power of mesmerism as well, which made him all the more dangerous, for he used his gift to cause pain and suffering."

His body rip—

"So you see, Jessamine, your father's blood runs within your veins. He was powerful, as Balthazar told you, and now his gift has awakened in you." She pauses, and her lips tighten. "That is why you must decide."

Something stirs within me at this moment: Pride. A desire for vengeance. Fear.

Alexander was one of our strongest members . . .

A malevolent group that lived in darkness and fed on fear . . .

But when they killed your father . . .

"I will stay," I tell her. "I will stay and fight."

Mother smiles, and it is a sad smile, but I sense resolution, too. *Is she relieved that I have accepted my fate?* She hugs me to her chest. "My dear child," she murmurs, gently stroking my head.

"But you'll stay too, won't you?" I plead, breaking our embrace. "Together. We're doing this together—right, Mother?"

She does not have to speak, for I see the answer in her eyes, but she does anyway. "My work is done now, child. As Balthazar said, it is time for a new generation to stop the evil that is stirring in the shadows."

My breath catches, and tears fill my eyes. "No, Mother," I protest. "I cannot do it without you."

She lifts my chin. "Within you lies strength yet to be discovered, Jess. Like your father . . . and your mother. Never forget that."

I bid her farewell an hour later.

I will be on my own. I said I would stay and fight.

What overcame me?

Now I sense the weight of those words, a promise I cannot break.

I wait with Mother on the railway platform. Balthazar has already said his farewell and now stands a few steps away to give us one more moment alone. There is a nip in the air, and the coolness I feel on my skin is a balm to the heat that spreads in my chest. Red and orange leaves swirl on the ground and up into the air. Mother takes my hands in hers. "Be safe, my child."

I sniffle, but hold back my tears.

"Remember," she says—and I glimpse that fierceness I saw when she cracked the lash—"you are your father's daughter, Jess."

Jess.

I hear the whistle of the train and the screech of the wheels. My eyes are misting over, but I try to be strong for her—and Papa.

A moment later she is gone. Balthazar comes to stand beside me. "Cora and Alexander could not have asked for a braver daughter," he says, looking down the tracks. A lingering wisp of smoke rises higher and higher until it disappears. "There is no greater cause than to destroy evil where it breeds."

I agree, but deep down inside, I wonder if I have made the right choice.

CHAPTER EIGHT

The League of Ravens

A knock at the door awakens me. Sunlight streams in through the cracked window. For a moment I don't know where I am, until I look around the small room and get my bearings. I'm in London, here to fight necromancers.

And then I remember.

Mother.

I have never spent a day without seeing her. It is a strange feeling, this distance between us. Whatever is to come, I hope it is resolved quickly and things will soon return to how they were.

"Who is it?" I call, rising from bed.

"Emily," a voice rings out.

I walk to the door in my nightdress and open it a crack. It is indeed Emily, with her white-blond hair and startling blue eyes. "Balthazar wants you," she says.

I find this rather impolite, but nod reflexively and close the door. My clothes are becoming quite spoiled, but I have no other option than to wear the ones I arrived in. Perhaps Mother will be able to send some of my favorite things from home.

I walk down the stairs slowly, wondering what this is all about. My heart flutters as I step into the sitting room.

"So you have arisen," Balthazar greets me, rising from the table. "I trust you slept well?"

"I did," I say, although I did not. The bed has left a creak in my back. "Thank you."

He gestures toward the table laden with food: toast and jam, bowls of porridge, a rasher of ham, a few withered-looking apples—and tea, of course. We are in England, after all. There does not seem to be a proper dining room—just the sitting room and the parlor—so this area must suffice as one. My former governess would be horrified.

I take a seat between Emily and Gabriel and reach for a slice of toast. Gabriel sits quietly and drinks his tea with careful sips, his little black book next to him. He does give me a slight smile, however, more so than upon our first meeting.

Progress, I think. Emily says nothing but attacks the food as if she is famished.

After breakfast, Balthazar calls us into the parlor, where a fire is burning in the grate. He eyes each of us in turn. *What is he doing?* I wonder. It seems like forever before he finally speaks. "Now that the three of you are here," he begins, "I want you to hear a tale."

Emily and Gabriel sit cross-legged by the fire, as if it is story time. I take a seat, and with the sound of a crackling fire as accompaniment, Balthazar begins his story.

"Many years ago, here in London lived a man named Malachai Grimstead. He had a brilliant and clever mind and was known in the scientific and medical communities of the day as a keen scholar. Indeed, he was a friend, and we often spent hours discussing the merits of science and philosophy."

"Did he know you was a faerie?" Emily asks. The heat from the fire on her face has turned her cheeks as red as apples.

"He did not, Emily. He was a man of science and intellect. It would have been too fantastical a story for him, and I did not want to explain or prove the existence of my kind to anyone."

He says this rather fiercely, and his eyes take on a sudden gleam.

"As the years passed, our friendship waned, for Malachai began to delve into subjects I found . . . revolting."

He pauses, as if waiting.

"What subjects?" I finally ask.

Balthazar leans forward in his chair and lowers his voice, as if relishing the horror of his tale. "The dead."

There is a moment of silence.

"Malachai believed that mankind did not live up to its fullest potential. He wanted to conquer death, to travel planes of existence that no man or woman had imagined. So from that day on, he began to take an obscene interest in the dead. He even hired resurrection men to do his dirty work."

"Resurrection men?" I ask.

Balthazar frowns with disapproval. "Grave robbers."

I feel as if I may faint.

"Soon, word spread of his nefarious activities. He was dismissed by the many societies that once looked to him for his curious mind and medical knowledge, and he retreated into the shadows."

Another pause. Balthazar sighs. "Malachai became . . . obsessed with the idea of bringing the dead back to life. He found others who shared his views, and together they traveled a path that led to death and despair. They called themselves Mephisto, a variation of the word 'Mephistopheles.'"

"The devil," Gabriel hisses.

"Yes, Gabriel. A demon from an old German legend called Faust, about a man who makes a pact with the devil."

"Did these people succeed?" Gabriel asks. His voice is deep and sounds strange coming from such a slight child. "In bringing back the dead?"

"They did. But what they brought back contained only a glimmer of human life. They were ghouls, undead creatures who exist only to do the bidding of their masters."

My stomach turns. This is ghastly, and I wonder once more if I should have returned home with Mother, but Balthazar continues, and I am swept back into the tale.

"The deeper Malachai delved, the more insane he became. He used these ghouls to capture human hosts for his experiments, and woe to the poor souls who fell into his trap.

"When bodies started showing up in the Thames—the discarded refuse of his vile work—the League of Ravens had no choice but to act. Malachai was killed, along with several of his followers." Balthazar looks at me. "It was Jessamine's father, Alexander Grace, who delivered the fatal blow."

Emily looks at me and *smiles*. I am taken aback, for this deed of Father's, albeit necessary, does not seem to be something to revel in.

Balthazar leans back in his chair and blows out a breath. "That was several years ago. But now, out of the shadows they have come again. They have made themselves known to Miss Jessamine and her mother."

"How?" Emily asks.

"They sent a message on a spirit slate, a tool to contact the dead."

"What was it?" Gabriel asks.

Balthazar looks to me. I swallow and, not for the last time, I am sure, repeat the strange words. "'Ring around the rosy, a pocketful of posies. Ashes! Ashes! We all fall down!'"

Emily screws up her face.

"Signed with the letter *M*," Balthazar adds, "as a dire warning."

He rises from his chair. "You were each chosen because you possess a special gift. One that can help destroy this menace. Beginning today, we must prepare. But first, Miss Jessamine, if you will stand, please."

I do as he bids. Gabriel and Emily stand also, and Gabriel draws the curtains shut.

Odd, that.

The room darkens but for the faint light that seeps through the curtains. Balthazar lights a candelabra with a match. Emily and Gabriel stand on either side of him. Everyone looks somber. "What is happening?" I ask.

But no one answers.

Balthazar walks to the corner of the room and picks up a long, wooden staff. A gleaming metal point shines at its tip. I hadn't even noticed it before—or perhaps I had mistaken it for a broom, which, judging from the dust on the floor, this room could certainly use. He walks back over and stands between Emily and Gabriel. They are all facing me, as if I am about to be questioned. *What is this about?*

Balthazar takes a step forward, so he is only a foot away. I feel sweat on my back. *It is unseemly for a lady to sweat,* I hear Mother's voice remind me.

"We are known as the League of Ravens," he announces, "named for Brân the Blessed, once king of Britain and protector of the realm."

My ears prick up. Although I did not finish my schooling, I certainly learned all of the British kings. Yet the name is unfamiliar. "Brân the Blessed? I have never heard of such a man."

"It is from the old Welsh tales," Balthazar replies, "the *Mabinogion,* in particular, which is now lost in history. *Brân* means 'raven' in the old tongue, and it is from him that we draw our strength."

I nod, enthralled.

"Since our order was formed, we have all sworn an oath to uphold its secrets. Now this duty falls upon you, Miss Jessamine."

He takes a step closer. A scent of deep woods and fallen leaves surrounds him, something I hadn't noticed before.

"Jessamine Grace. Do you come here of your own free will, being of sound mind?"

I take a breath. "I do."

"And do you swear to use your gift for the good of

mankind and strike down evil at any cost, even at risk to your own life?"

My legs quake.

"I do."

"Furthermore, will you hold the practices of this order in confidence and not betray its members, secrets, or powers to any dark force that may exist in this world?"

"I will," I say.

Balthazar raises the spear to my throat so quickly, I gasp. "Swear to me now, child." His face is stern, and his eyes gleam with a fierce light.

"I swear," I finish.

Balthazar drops the staff to his side. "Jessamine Grace, daughter of Alexander and Cora, welcome to the League of Ravens." He raises one hand in front of my face and makes an intricate motion in the air.

A shock runs through my body.

I see a silver ship with a billowing sail, rocking gently on the sea . . .

A white raven pecking at a ravished corpse on a hillside.

Creatures with ghoulish faces burned by fire.

And a giant of a man, swinging a shining sword above his head.

As quickly as it comes, the vision is over. I shake my head, disoriented.

"They are glimpses of our past," Balthazar explains.

"Something you will now carry forever. In times of great peril, you will never be alone."

He steps back two paces. "All hail!" he proclaims, and bangs the staff to the floor three times, sending a shudder down my spine.

The serious faces from a moment ago are now all smiles. Balthazar reaches out and takes my hand. "Welcome to the order, Jess."

Jess. It is the first time he has used my pet name.

"Thank you," I say, surprised, still reeling from the vision. "I'm honored."

"I am glad you are with us," Gabriel says. His words are a comfort, but his eyes are dark. He looks weary beyond his years. *Will this happen to me, also?*

Emily grasps my hand. Her touch is so light, I almost don't feel it. "We're best mates now. Yeah?"

I smile, and feel a tickle at my throat. I touch it, and when I draw my hand away, a smear of blood darkens my fingertip.

Emily looks at me and shrugs. "Just a scratch," she says.

CHAPTER NINE

Power Revealed

I am now a member of the League of Ravens.

I swore to it. Upon penalty of death.

I feel a bond with Mother and Father that I have never known before. They went through this same initiation. How I wish to ask Mother what she felt at the time. What did she think? Was she frightened? What adventures did she and Father share?

I will write to her soon, I promise myself, for there is so much more I want to know.

. . .

Over the next several days, Balthazar teaches me how to use the lash. We are in the back garden, where a broken-down carriage sits. One of its wheels is cracked, and the spokes are either bent or missing. Brambles and vines run wild back here, looking as if they might rise up and strangle the entire house. The air is cool, but with my cloak and gloves, I am warm and flushed. Emily has lent me a few things to wear, but they are rather small and uncomfortable.

"Grip the handle lightly," Balthazar says for the second time. "Raise your arm above your head. Now strike!"

I lash out at the dressmaker's form that he has furnished for practice. I walk a few steps and peer at the damage. The spiked ends of the whip have torn the roughspun cloth, shredding it in places. I can't imagine what it would do to a real body. And then it hits me: that is why I am doing this. The enemy we fight is *real*. This lash is meant to kill. Before I have a chance to obsess on this further, Balthazar congratulates me.

"Better," he says. "That's better, Jess. You will find that the lash has a few tricks of its own, too."

"What do you mean?"

"When it is used in battle, it knows the touch of evil, and works to defeat it."

Good, I think. *I'll need all the help I can get.*

We work on my stance next, feet planted apart, eyes and ears alert.

And then the most curious thing happens.

Balthazar seems to be in several places at once, disappearing in an instant and then reappearing. I know he is not *really* disappearing, but within the blink of an eye, he is in front of me and then behind me. Now he is at my side.

"Just a touch of glamour," he says. "It will sharpen your senses."

"What is glamour?"

"It is the art of illusion, something all of my race are gifted with."

He is now standing on my other side. I didn't even see him move.

"Try to strike," he orders me. "Anticipate my movements."

I grip the handle of the lash as he appears several feet away. I strike out, but too late. Now he is behind me. I can sense him. I turn quickly, but my feet are swept out from under me. I'm falling, but before I hit the ground, I regain my balance, spin on my heel, and lash out with the whip, which tangles around Balthazar's ankle.

"There's the spirit!" he encourages me. "Well done."

I snap the lash back and the thongs unfurl from his boot. I feel beads of sweat on my face. It is unseemly for a lady to sweat. *Says who?* I think, and turn quickly, lashing out at the dressmaker's form again.

• • •

Before I retire to bed, Balthazar calls me into the sitting room. He stands up as I enter and offers his hand as an invitation to sit, which I do, directly across from him. "A mesmerist's power can be a strong force, Jessamine," he begins. "The mysteries of one's mind can be laid open and observed to great detriment."

I don't answer, only nod. He crosses his legs at the knee. "I am curious about your gift and would like to try an experiment."

"Certainly," I tell him.

"You have to trust me, though," he says slyly. "Do you trust me, Jess?"

Quite frankly, I'm still not sure how I feel about Balthazar. *Didn't faeries steal young maidens in the stories—never to be seen or heard from again?*

The thought is unsettling. *But he is a friend of Mother's and Father's,* I tell myself. He would not harm me. *Except for the spear at my throat.* "Yes," I say, nonetheless. "I trust you."

He smiles and reaches inside his jacket. I tense for a moment, but he only withdraws a length of narrow black cloth. "I will bind this around your eyes so you cannot see. I will then ask you several questions. Does that meet with your approval?"

I nod.

He stands up and walks behind me, then places the cloth over my eyes and ties it at the back. Darkness. I hear his footsteps as he walks back to his side of the table. A match is struck. The acrid scent of sulfur fills my nostrils, then the waxy smell of tallow as a candle is lit.

"Is it too tight?" he asks.

I blink underneath the cloth. "No," I answer.

What is he up to?

I hear a drawer sliding open and the clink and clatter of objects being placed on the table. "Jessamine," he begins, "there are three things in front of you. I'm going to touch each one, and I want you to tell me what it is."

I nod and let out a breath. The woodsy smell that surrounds Balthazar is stronger now, as if being sightless makes my other senses more keen.

"Now," he says. "What am I touching?"

I breathe in and sense something hard in my mind's eye, like an impenetrable wall or an ominous standing stone.

"A rock?" I venture.

Balthazar doesn't answer, only says, "And this?"

Something soft and delicate, like a cloud or a pillow, appears in the darkness. I can almost feel it under my fingertips. "That's a silk cloth."

"Does it have a color?"

"Red," I answer immediately.

I realize I can almost sense Balthazar smiling. All I have to do is concentrate, and the pictures come to me.

"And one more," he urges.

This one brings a strange sensation, as if I am being watched. It roams over me, and I feel exposed, as if something is looking into my very soul. "An . . . eye?" I guess, although I have no idea how that can be possible.

Balthazar's chair scrapes the floor, and I hear his footsteps as he comes to stand behind me again. He gently unties the knot of the blindfold and returns to his seat. I blink several times at the candlelight and then look at the objects on the table. There is a black stone—that was the first object. The second is a small square of silk cloth with a pattern of red roses stitched into the fabric. I look down the length of the table again. "Where's the other thing?" I ask. "The last one?"

Balthazar taps a long finger at the corner of his eye. "That was my eye," he says. "For I will always be watching."

I don't know whether this is a reassuring thought or not.

"Looking into another's mind is an invasion," he tells me, "and can be a dangerous journey. The seeker opens herself up and is vulnerable to attack. One can become lost in another's thoughts, as if in a maze, and never find her way out again. Do you understand?"

"Yes," I say, although I am thinking of something else. "My father. Tell me of him. You were . . . close?"

Balthazar seems taken aback, but then a sad smile forms on his face. This is not a question he expected, I would assume. "Alexander was a dear friend and colleague," he says. "Brave, generous, and always the first to rush into battle." His smile broadens a little, perhaps at the memory of better times.

"How did he die?"

He exhales a weary breath. "Mephisto laid a trap, with your mother as the quarry. I told Alexander to wait—that we needed to think it through. But his love for her could not be swayed by logic. He rushed in too quickly, and there, he met his end."

Anger wells up inside of me. "But he did not die in vain," I insist, looking for solace. "He killed one of them. Malachai Grimstead. You said that he delivered the killing blow."

"That is true, Jessamine. And soon after, Mephisto fled into the shadows."

"Until now," I say.

"Yes, my child. Until now."

My left hand tightens into a fist. I think of the gentle father I knew, and see another side of him, that of a fierce warrior. *Always the first to rush into battle.*

"Already I can see his bravery in you, Jessamine," Balthazar says. "And your mother's."

I unclench my fist. *Yes,* I think. *I see it too.*

Silence fills the room.

"Is there anything else?" he asks, and his eyebrows rise, as if he has a secret waiting to be revealed.

I search my thoughts. He seems to be referring to something specific, but what? "No," I say, although it is more of a question.

Balthazar leans forward in his chair a little and sweeps his hair away from his face. "There is always a consequence when using an ability. One that varies from person to person, but still, there is always a cost."

Now I realize. I think back on the few times I have used the gift of mesmerism: the man on the bus or reading Emily's mind. Each time ended with a feeling of fatigue.

"I didn't know you noticed," I say.

Balthazar only points to his eye again.

"I feel tired after I do it. It's a sharp pain along my neck and shoulders, sometimes even a stab in my temple. What is it?"

"The power of mesmerism uses energies that can exhaust one's spirit. Use it carefully, Jess. One would not want to be drained of power when it is needed most."

I find this thought disturbing and rub my temple with two fingers, as I feel a headache coming on.

I am exhausted, and my hand throbs from gripping the lash. After leaving Balthazar, I pass Emily's room on the way to my own. A faint glow pulses along the bottom of her door. Strange, that. It's evening now, but I don't smell wood smoke or the oil from a lamp. I knock and then enter.

My mouth opens in shock.

Emily is sitting on her bed, tossing a ball of light from hand to hand.

"Emily!" I shout.

She looks up, and there is not the slightest hint of fear on her face.

"It's only light," she says. "That's my power. I'm a light-bringer."

I close the door and take a step closer. White and yellow trails swirl about in the ball.

"A what? What is — Can you feel it? Is it hot?"

"Not now," she says, "but if I get angry . . ."

She closes her eyes. A vein begins to throb at her temple. The ball of light is turning, changing to a fiery red. A bead of sweat appears on her forehead.

"Emily," I say, "are you all right?"

She opens her eyes. The orb returns to a cool yellow and then vanishes right before my eyes. She releases a tremulous breath, and we are in the dark. I hear her fumbling at the table by her bed and then the strike of a match. Candlelight brightens the room, but it is faint. She stands and lights a wall sconce so we have more to see by, and then sits back down on the bed.

"How?" I ask her. "Could you always do this?"

"When I was a wee child, I remember me mum blowing out the candle at my bedside. When she left the room, I lit my own light. I thought everybody could do it."

I feel sad at hearing these words.

"One day I got mad 'cause me old da' beat me for stealing food. I got so angry, the house almost burned down. After that, he took me away."

A vision of Emily being dragged up the street flashes through my mind. My heart breaks. She was misunderstood and given away out of fear.

"For a long time after that, I couldn't make my light anymore, but old Balthy taught me how to control it, see?"

"Old Balthy?"

"Yeah," she says. "Old Balthy. What kind of name *is* Balthazar, anyway?"

"I don't know," I answer vaguely. There is silence for a moment. "How do you feel about all this?" I ask her, peering about the room.

"All what?"

"Being here in London. Living in this house. This League of Ravens business."

"Oh," she says casually. "Well, the way I see it, there's good blokes and bad ones, right? I seen lots of 'em at the orphanage. And this Mephisto is bad. They killed your da', didn't they?"

Emily's cavalier mention of Father's passing takes me by surprise. Balthazar must have told her. "Yes," I say. "They did."

"Well then, it sounds like you've got to revenge him."

"Yes," I agree. "I surely think so."

Emily gestures for me to sit, which I do, in a small, child-like chair next to her desk.

"It was just me and Gabbyshins at the orphanage," she starts, fiddling with the stitched fabric of her bedding. "We had to look after ourselves. A sorry lot they all were. And the food! Blimey! Mush every day."

"Mush?"

"Well, mush is the same as slop, but mush has peas. Sometimes we'd get a wrinkled piece of meat."

"Who is Gabbyshins?"

"Gabriel," she explains. "Old Gabbyshins, I call him."

We are interrupted by a knock at the door. To my surprise, Gabriel enters.

"Speak of the devil, and he will appear," Emily says.

Gabriel narrows his eyes at her.

"Sorry," she mutters, sinking back into the bed.

I find this exchange between the two of them very odd.

"I told her," Emily goes on. "I told her about my light."

Gabriel closes the door behind him and stands, as there is no place for him to sit other than the foot of the bed. I study his face. There is something sad there, behind the dark circles of his eyes, like he's carrying the burden of the world on his small shoulders. *But why would a young boy have this look about him?* "I guess you want to know about me, then," he says.

Yes! I think, but do not let my curiosity show.

He walks to the small window and stares out at the dark. I watch his shoulders rise and fall. He reaches into his coat, and when he turns back around, a small stringed instrument is cradled in his arms. It is then that I hear perhaps the loveliest sound I have ever heard. It fills me with a sense of joy, and all in the world seems to be at ease. I close my eyes. I see Mother and Father laughing. I see myself and Deepa down at the docks, watching the ships come in.

And then Gabriel plays another note.

The joy vanishes, to be replaced by a sense of loss I feel in the pit of my stomach. It is painful—not in a physical way, but an ache, as if my soul itself has been pierced. He strikes another note, and the pain subsides.

Emily smiles. "Neat, innit?"

I gaze at Gabriel, and the candlelight flickers on his face.

"Are you all right?" he asks.

"Y-yes—" I stutter. "That—instrument. What is it? What are you?"

"Merely a bard," he says, "and this is only a harp."

97

Emily giggles, as if sharing in a private joke.

"My gift lies in the power to affect others through song," Gabriel says. "I can change people's emotions and even drive them to do terrible things."

"Fascinating," I murmur. But I wonder if there's more to his story, and I try to look into his mind. I know it is an invasion, but I keep my gaze steady. I sense nothing, like I am staring at a blank white canvas. He looks at me curiously until I turn away, embarrassed, and feel the telltale pain along my shoulders.

"And is that *all* you can do?" I ask.

Emily laughs. "I think that's quite enough, innit? You shoulda seen what he done to old Olly back at Nowhere, just by playing a song on that there harp."

"Nowhere?" I ask.

"The orphanage," Gabriel clarifies. "That's what we called it."

Nowhere, I think. What dreadful things could one witness at such a place? I don't have to ask aloud, because Emily tells me. "There were a man named Fitchett what roamed around at night with a silver cane," she says, "tapping the floors to make sure we was snug in bed. You'd hear him coming: *tap, tap, tap.* He smelled like gin and old onions."

I imagine that the two of them must have had quite a hard time at the orphanage.

"And how do you feel about all this?" I ask Gabriel, just

as I did Emily. "Being here, under Balthazar's charge? This League of Ravens?"

Gabriel does not hesitate. "It is my duty to strike down evil wherever it may stand. Only through light can the darkness be vanquished."

"That just means he'll slay any beastie we come across," Emily says.

Gabriel shakes his head, but I see a smile in his dark eyes.

The three of us, I think. *Together—the League of Ravens.*

Whatever is to come, I am not alone.

CHAPTER TEN

The Rosy Boy

M y first real outing into London comes the next day.
Balthazar has asked Emily and Gabriel to show me the
market so I can become a little more familiar with my
surroundings. "You need to know your way around if you're
ever on the run," he had said, his face showing no sign of
humor.

This gives me pause, but I do feel the need to explore. I
could use a break from the training.

Once we depart, I discover that the East End of London is beyond anything I could have prepared for. Children
with no shoes on their feet run around like packs of wild

animals, people wheel carts of food down muddy streets, pigs and cows meander in back gardens, and horse-drawn carriages rumble along so quickly, I have to dive out of the way. Worst of all, factories belch clouds of black smoke into the air.

But that is nothing compared with the market itself, which is only a few short blocks from 17 Wadsworth Place. The High Street, Emily calls it.

"Filthy" is too kind a word for this place. Vagabonds are at every other step, holding out battered hats for money. A few mean-looking women stand in front of their doors dressed only in thin smallclothes. Some men lie drunk amidst the stench and rubbish. Chickens squawk, sheep bleat, and placid cows move along slowly, as if they know what their fate will be. My leather boots are immediately ruined by some unknown murky substance that I fear is animal blood from a butcher's shop. It is horrendous. Emily and Gabriel, however, seem to take no notice, as if this is just another jolly trip to the market.

The day is cold but sunny, and the three of us weave our way among the stalls, where costermongers sell everything from bread and meat to roasted chestnuts. The air is full of chattering voices and sharp smells. Songbirds shriek inside their cages. And everywhere hawkers crying their wares:

"Sheep's trotters! One guinea!"

"Potato! All hot! Potatoes here!"

"Hot eels! Ha'penny!"

A young boy, his face darkened by what looks like coal, sweeps a path in the dirty street, hoping for a few coins from a kind stranger. Gathering my skirts, I quickly step around a mound of horse muck. So far, I find this adventure absolutely appalling.

"Oh!" Emily cries, and suddenly stops.

"What is it?" I ask, looking around warily, perhaps for one of Mephisto's ghouls.

"I smell eel pie," she says, a hungry gleam in her eyes. "C'mon. Nothing better than a bit o' pie and mash."

The thought of eel *anything* revolts me, but I follow her and Gabriel as she winds her way among the vendors. After a moment we find ourselves at a stall where pies are set out on a wooden slab. Emily licks her lips. The pie man leans over the makeshift counter. I shrink back. "Don't think I can't see ye," he mutters, "just because me gots only one eye."

I force myself to look at his face. Where his left eye should be is a scarred flap of dry skin. A red neckerchief is knotted around his throat.

"How much for the eel pie, then?" Emily asks.

He mutters something I cannot hear and winks at her with his good eye. He looks at me for an uncomfortably long moment. "And what are you lot doing out all on your lonesome?"

"Piss off," Emily says sharply, and I gasp at her language. "Just give us the pie, then, yeah?"

"Har! She's a sassy one!" he bellows, revealing teeth the color of mud. He lifts a pie and pokes a crooked finger through the crusty top, then holds it up and licks it. "Ah," he moans. "Cat."

I close my eyes.

He picks up another, but this time, he digs in with two fingers and pulls out what must surely be an eel. He tilts back his head and opens his mouth, and as I watch in horror, the eel slides down his throat with a disgusting slurp. "Mmm," he says. "Fishy. That'll be your eel, then."

My stomach falls to my feet.

He lifts the pie tin and hands it to Emily, who drops a few coins into his hand. *She's going to buy it? After he put his grubby fingers into it!*

He tosses the coins into an empty can, and then his horrid gaze falls on me again. The flap of skin that covers his eye socket twitches, as if an eyeball were still in there, moving around. Quicker than lightning, his hand shoots out and squeezes my wrist. "Better get home soon, poppet," he whispers. "When it gets dark here, bad things come out."

"Ow!" I shout. "Unhand me!"

Emily pulls me away. "Sod off, you great pillock!"

I would be shocked once again by Emily's language, but I am still reeling from the man's breath.

"C'mon," Gabriel says, a fierce look in his eyes. "Let's go."

I leave the stall shaking and glance back at the exact moment the pie vendor snorts into a yellow rag.

"You all right, then?" Emily asks.

I let out a bewildered breath. "Yes," I say. "What a beast!"

"Aw, that old codger's no trouble," she says. "Me and Gabbyshins had to put up with worse back at Nowhere."

The sound of an organ grinder drifts through the air. I look up to see that the clear sky has given over to threatening storm clouds. We continue on, passing the stalls and crowds, and come upon a ragged boy and girl sitting on blocks of wood, trying to earn a few coppers. A basket of hand-carved clothespins sits before them. They are both so skinny, my heart breaks just looking at them. Back in Deal, there were several poor families, but nothing compares to these two, with their sunken cheeks and scabby knees. They don't even have proper clothes. "C'mon," Emily urges me. "What are you lookin' at?"

"Nothing," I say, turning away from the two children, and wishing I had some coins to give. Before I can think on them any longer, the faint ringing of jaunty music rises in my ears, different from the organ grinder's. As we turn the corner, I see the source.

A little distance from the street, under a group of trees, several men and women are gathered. A few small children sit on blankets in front of a bow-topped caravan, a sort of wagon. A sorry-looking mule snuffs at the dry grass, and a skinny dog gnaws on a bone.

"Who are they?" I ask.

"Gypsies," Emily says.

Gabriel shakes his head. "They are called the Roma people. They fled faraway lands, where they were persecuted, only to arrive in England to suffer the same fate."

I am taken aback by Gabriel's serious tone. I look back at the group. The women are dressed in long, colorful skirts, with scarves on their heads, and the men in loose trousers and black boots. A big, burly man is the source of the music and plays a curious instrument with black and white keys like a piano but held up to his chest by a strap around his neck. Fingers as large as sausages nimbly work over the keys.

"C'mon, then," Emily says, tugging my hand. "Bloody pie's getting cold."

We continue on, the music fading, and pass a storefront with broken windows. A red X is painted on the door. "What is this?" I ask. We all pause and peer inside. It is a clockmaker's shop, and it is entirely disheveled. Tall tower clocks are toppled over,

gears and little springs are strewn about, and the counters
have been smashed. Shards of glass sparkle on the wooden
floor. I look back at the door. Underneath the X, there is a
handbill written in big block letters:

HUE & CRY!

A GREAT PUBLIC MEETING
OF THE WORKING CLASSES

9 NOVEMBER

COMMUNISTS!
IMMIGRANTS!
GYPSIES!

SPREADERS OF DISEASE
AND SICKNESS.
PROTECT YOUR FAIR
ENGLAND!

FOREIGNERS OUT!

"What's a communist?" Emily asks.

But I don't have a chance to answer, for right at that moment, a little boy stumbles out of the alley to our left. He doesn't wear a shirt or shoes, only ragged trousers cut off at the knee. We all pause. There is something wrong with him, I realize. He's sick. Red, weeping sores mark his chest.

"Help," the little boy whispers, thrusting out stiff black fingers, more like a claw than a hand. "Please. Help me."

I recall the dream I had the other night—a little girl in a pinafore dress, with blood along the hem. I take a step toward him.

"Wait!" Gabriel warns.

The boy steps closer. He swallows and then opens his mouth. *"Ring around the rosy,"* he sings weakly. *"A pocketful of posies. Ashes! Ashes! We all fall down!"*

And then he does exactly that, right there in the filthy alley.

CHAPTER ELEVEN

Upon a Silver Tray

The three of us stand several feet from the body, silent. The air is cooler now, and fine drops of rain begin to fall. Emily screws up her face. "Wouldn't wanna catch whatever's got to him."

"It's the same rhyme," I say, and my voice seems loud in the mouth of the alley, bouncing off the dank walls and back into my throat. "The same message that was written on the slate back home."

"Strange," Gabriel mutters. He takes a few hesitant steps closer but remains a safe distance away. After a moment he raises his right hand and makes the sign of the cross in the air. I hear his voice, deep yet soft, and the words drift into my ears. *"Requiem aeternam dona eis, Domine,"* he whispers.

A prayer?

Emily's voice brings me back to the moment. "We better get back," she says, "and tell old Balthy what happened."

"We can't just leave him here," I protest.

"We shouldn't get any closer," Gabriel says. "He has surely died."

"How can you tell?" I ask.

Gabriel turns to me, his dark eyes somber. "I just know," he says flatly.

"Right," Emily adds. "He would know."

I sigh in frustration. *"How* would you just know?"

But Gabriel doesn't answer, only lowers his head a moment and avoids my gaze.

Is this something to do with his power? The music?

I look once again at the boy's body.

"C'mon," Emily insists, taking my hand. "Let's be off."

I pull myself away, but as we head back to 17 Wadsworth Place, I hear the rhyme repeating in my head: *Ashes! Ashes! We all fall down!*

"It was just like the rhyme on the slate," I tell Balthazar. "The exact same words."

"He were dirty," Emily adds, "and all covered in rosy marks. His fingernails was all blacklike, sire."

We take refuge in the sitting room and warm ourselves before the fire. My clothes have become damp and itchy from the sudden rain. Balthazar sits quietly, but he looks as if he could spring into action at any moment. His brow furrows at our news. "It sounds like one of your nursery rhymes."

One of *your,* I notice. I sometimes forget that he is not fully human.

"But what does it mean?" I ask.

"That is still a mystery, Miss Jessamine, but it is surely the work of Mephisto."

He's right. There is no other reason why this same rhyme would be sung by the boy and also appear on the slate.

"He was ravaged by disease," Gabriel says. "Some terrible sickness."

"Be on your guard," Balthazar warns us. "If you see anyone like this again, do not go near them under any circumstance."

We all nod in agreement. There is a moment of silence that seems to go on forever.

"Bloody starving," Emily finally says. "Who wants some eel pie?"

I eat very little at dinner, only some cold ham and bread, while Gabriel and Emily share their eel pie. I have to admit, the pie did smell rather tempting as it warmed on the stove, but I could not bring myself to partake. The image of the Rosy Boy, as Emily calls him, remains in my head.

Balthazar seems content to nibble at pomegranate seeds. *What else does he eat?* I remember his graceful manners at table when Mother and I first visited him in the West End, but I recall nothing on his plate. Maybe it was some kind of faerie illusion. Maybe, in fact, he doesn't really eat at all.

I retire to my room but cannot escape the terrible scene from only a few hours ago. When the boy sang *"Ashes! Ashes!"* his voice had risen to a weak shout, as if trying to retch up whatever sickness he held in his body.

"Help," he had whispered. *"Please. Help me."*

But we did nothing.

What befell him? Is there someone out there now, searching the streets for any sign of him?

Gabriel said he was surely dead. But how would he know?

He whispered as he made the sign of the cross.

The words were familiar, but their meaning escaped me in that dire situation. Now it has come back. It is Latin, which I have heard at church with Mother, and also from my governess. *Requiem* means "rest," and *Domine* is "Lord."

Mother, I am reminded. I said I would write.

I find a quill, ink, and parchment at the small desk and sit down. By candlelight, I begin:

Dearest Mother,

I hope this finds you well. I am settling in here, albeit strangely. I have become friends with Emily and Gabriel and am now initiated into the League of Ravens. Oh! How I wish you were here, but I am carrying on, doing my best, and thinking of you often.

Today, the most curious thing happened. We saw a boy who sang the same rhyme that was on the spirit slate. He was in such a state, and I fear he may be dead. It is all connected, but as of yet we do not know how.

I do so long to see you again when we can put this terrible situation behind us.

Yours always,
Jess

For a moment I think to sign "Jessamine," but the quill stops on the last *s*.

I wait for the ink to dry before folding the parchment into thirds.

My sleep is filled with not just one child singing the rosy rhyme, but hundreds. They stumble along the dark streets, their clothes in tatters, their eyes vacant and bloodshot. And everywhere, the marks—livid welts that burn a feverish and angry red.

In the morning, I sit in the parlor and take my tea. Emily and Gabriel must be asleep, I surmise. I always rose early at home with Mother, and we would sit together and share breakfast. It seems as if this will always be my fate, that of an early riser.

The telltale click of Balthazar's boots brings me back to the moment. I turn from my breakfast as he enters. His face is drawn. He stands before me, bearing a silver tray in his hand. A letter is upon it. My heart rises. "From Mother?" I question.

He only smiles weakly. I take the envelope and use an ivory letter opener to break the wax seal. I stare at the words. I read them quickly, but they don't register. I read them again.

"It came late last night," he says. "I am so very sorry, my child."

I look back to the letter.

Deal, Kent, England
November, 1864

Miss Jessamine Grace,

It is with the deepest sorrow that I must inform you of the murder of Mrs. Cora Grace, who was killed by unknown assailants in Deal two nights ago. Constables are searching for clues, which, at the moment, are few.

   We commend her soul to the Father of Mercies and the God of all consolation. Please accept my sincerest condolence under this sad bereavement.

I remain, your loyal servant.

Frederick Warburton, Constable
Deal, Kent County, England

The letter falls from my hands. "No," I whisper.

Balthazar lays a hand on my shoulder. "We will avenge her, Jessamine. That I promise you."

"No," I say again.

And then the tears come.

PART TWO

The Great Calamity

CHAPTER TWELVE

A Hall of Grief

There is a bleakness to the landscape that seems more melancholy than ever: the bare, stunted trees; the sky so gray, one aches for the sun . . .

Mother is dead.

Dead.

Surely killed by Mephisto.

I make a promise to myself.

I will destroy them, even if it kills me, too. The black mourning band I wear on my arm is a testament to her memory.

The trip back to Deal for the funeral is a blur. Balthazar accompanies me and looks after all the important details—finding the mourning house to be fitted for a dress, sending the funeral invitations, and contacting the local parish.

I am awake but asleep, a ghost floating in a space that has no beginning or end, just an endless hall of grief.

We devise a ruse in which Balthazar has become my uncle and I his ward back in London. "Uncle B," I call him, although this is met by skepticism from some of our neighbors. Fortunately, Mother and I had mostly kept to ourselves, other than our appointments with those seeking to connect with their loved ones, and no one would dare ask for more information on such a solemn occasion. The English are too polite, at least on the surface.

"*Poor child,*" I hear more than once.

"*She's only a babe.*"

"*First the father, now the mother.*"

"*Such a shame.*"

And here in the parish amidst the mourners, I see several of our former clients, including Dr. Barnes, whose face is still as shattered as it was when the message was revealed on the spirit slate. I feel a sense of loathing. What Mother and I had been doing—our charade of contacting the dead—was wicked. *How could we have played on people's sorrows?*

Before the service, Balthazar and I talk to the chief

inspector and the physician. "She did not suffer," the physician tells us. "She was found by one of her clients when he rang for an appointment. All signs point to intruders, although there was no sign of theft."

"How did she . . . die?" I ask, somehow gaining the courage.

Balthazar lays a hand on my shoulder.

The chief inspector, who wears epaulets with three shining stars on his uniform, seems taken aback. He looks to Balthazar—ignoring me, for I am only a child—and my blood boils.

"Sir," the inspector begins, "perhaps it's best if we speak alo—"

"No," I cut him off. "Tell me."

He shakes his head slightly when he sees no admonition from Balthazar, and then blows out a breath that smells of the gin palace. After a moment he speaks, but although he is addressing me, his eyes drift to Balthazar on every other word. "Oddest thing it were. Her body did not bear any marks of violence, but . . . well—"

He fumbles again, as if searching for the right words, or ones delicate enough for a young lady's ears. Balthazar's calm demeanor flares. "Out with it, sir!"

Several heads turn our way, and even I jump at his tone. The inspector rakes a hand through his thinning hair and lowers his voice. "Well, sir, there were no signs of injury to her body, but it was under mysterious circumstances."

"*What* mysterious circumstances?" I ask, although I am not sure I want the answer.

The chief inspector looks to me and then to Balthazar, still unsure of whom to address. "Well, that's the strange thing, isn't it? The letter *M*. It were written on the floor . . . in blood."

Now there is no doubt.

Mother was killed by Mephisto.

I recall our first meeting with Balthazar and hear her words as if they were spoken yesterday: *Your father and I were instrumental in stopping Mephisto in the past. They will surely seek retribution.*

The train from Deal to Charing Cross was late, and I am terribly exhausted. I feel as if I may faint from fatigue and the trauma of this whole trip. Balthazar hailed a hansom cab from the station, and now we sit next to each other as it winds its way throughout the London streets. A slight rain has begun to fall. Balthazar gives me his coat, and I wrap myself in my own sadness, barely finding the strength to speak. "They will come after me next," I tell him. "I am my father's daughter."

"I will not let that happen," he promises me. "I owe it to Alexander and your mother." He pauses, and in the dark light of the carriage I feel tension rising from his body. "I should have taken more caution!" he says sharply. "Cora was not safe, and I sent her back without any foresight to danger. I promise you, Jess. Her death will not be in vain."

His words do not soothe me, and I pull the coat tighter around me, hoping somehow to suffocate the pain I feel. It does not work, and before I know it, I have fallen asleep.

I awake a short time later, and we are still traveling. I look out into the night sky. A few stars wink in a canopy of black. Balthazar notices my gaze. "The stars tell a story tonight," he says.

"You read the stars?" I ask him.

"In a way. My kind are close to nature. We can sense the earth and its moods—starlight, the tides, the very air we breathe."

"Tell me," I implore him, desiring anything that will brighten my thoughts. "Tell me of your world."

His eyes twinkle, cool and silver. "I will, my child. But not now, for it is a long story, and perhaps best told on another night than this."

But then he begins to sing quietly, and as the carriage rattles along, his words rise over the creaking wheels:

> "Awake, dear child and gaze upon the land, from
>   these boughs on high:
> beechen white and towering ash, sycamore and dew.
> Lay your gentle head upon these leaves . . ."

But that is all I hear, for my head bobs upon my chest, and within a minute I fall once more into a deep slumber.

I awake the morning after my return to 17 Wadsworth Place to find that Darby has been called here from SummerHall to "look after Master," as she tells me. She arrives laden with two trunks. I look through them and, to my amazement, find several dresses, pairs of boots, and other assorted items. I also see the spirit board, the one I used upon first meeting Balthazar. I still remember the smoky black words hovering above his head: "rose," "dawn," "aurora."

"Go on, then, miss," Darby urges me. "They're yours."

"How?" I ask her. "Where did these things come from?"

"Master bade me find some clothes for the lady, miss, so I went shopping in the Mayfair High Street. Even told me to buy one for meself, he did." She smiles, the first time I have ever seen her do so, revealing crooked teeth.

These clothes are a luxury I could never afford. I was able to pack a few small things from home when Balthazar and I were in Deal—but perhaps he is just trying to bring a smile to my face and ease my sadness.

There is a chill I feel deep down to my bones.

Later that evening, Darby comes in to stoke the fire. She kneels before the hearth to tend the kindling, and I take the opportunity to study her.

She is a werewolf. How is that possible?

Patches of moonlight spill through the window and onto the hardwood floor. If it were full, what would happen? *Would she drop to her knees and scream? Would she howl and grimace and run rampant through the house? Would she come after me?*

Not that I'm frightened of her. Balthazar seems to trust her in the presence of others. In a moment I hear the crackling of tinder, and small wisps of smoke rise from the hearth. Darby stands up and puts her irons into a bucket. I wonder how she can be near flames after what she has been through. "Will there be anything else, miss?" she asks.

"No, Darby," I say, in as friendly a tone as I can muster. "Thank you."

She dips her head and walks quietly to the door.

Then she stops.

For a very long moment she is still. Finally she turns around. "It were a fire," she says.

I feel as if a cold bucket of water has been poured over my head. *Did she notice my stares?* I am at a loss for words, but then—"Does it hurt?"

"Not anymore, miss. It did once. Long ago."

She raises her free hand, the bucket of tools in the other, and, as if in a trance, absently strokes the white scars on her face.

A young girl, lashed to a cross, with flames roaring around her.

"Thank you for telling me," I say.

"It's fine, miss."

"Call me Jess," I say firmly. "I insist."

"Fine, miss," she repeats, doing nothing of the sort, and steps out quietly, closing the door behind her.

Before I drift off to sleep, Emily creeps into my room. To my surprise, she lies down on the bed and puts her small arms around me. For a moment she says nothing, and I imagine this is what it must feel like to have a sister, sharing nightly visits and quiet secrets. "I'm sorry, Jess," she finally says. "We'll make them bogeys pay for what they done."

And then the tears come again. But within seconds I feel heat spreading out from her tiny body, which warms my cold hands and my spirit as well.

CHAPTER THIRTEEN

A Light Shining Bright

My fingers hover above the spirit board.

I have seen it before, the night Mother and I first met Balthazar, but now I look more closely. The sun and moon are placed at the top left and right, and two pyramids, each with an all-seeing eye, anchor the bottom. Most chilling of all is a golden skull in the center, flanked by wings. The alphabet is carved in lustrous gold.

We are gathered around the parlor table. A fire blazes in the hearth, for the gray afternoon is cold, and the chill seems to creep through the doors and windows. Emily and Gabriel sit to either side of me, Balthazar at the head.

"Each time you have used your gift," Balthazar begins, "the subject has been close at hand. The first was when you and your mother came to visit."

I absently touch the planchette while listening, my thoughts scattered.

"The second," he continues, "if I remember correctly, was with the man on the omnibus."

I look up from the board. "I thought—how did you—"

"My kind is sensitive to any supernatural qualities," Balthazar explains, "or what some would call magic. I was aware of it immediately."

Seems right, I muse. *He is a faerie, after all.*

"And your third time was with Emily, when you saw her early life."

I nod in agreement. Emily gives me a small smile.

"Your most recent, if memory serves, was when you were blindfolded. But this time is different. Our subject is not here, so you will not see the smoke—the thought made solid, which you have seen before—so I want you to think on the *idea* of your mother. Bring it to the front of your mind and try to find anything that can tell us what befell her."

I let out a breath.

"Now," Balthazar says, "join hands. Everyone."

I am taken aback, as I thought I would use the planchette to find words through the spirit board.

"It will still guide us, Jessamine," Balthazar says, as if

reading my thoughts. He waves his hand over the board. The letters and symbols blur. I hear Emily's intake of breath.

"It is not a traditional spirit board," Balthazar explains, "but something of an entirely different sort."

I look back to the board, which is swirling with mist that hovers above the surface. After a moment it fades, and I am staring into a watery reflection of my own face.

"It is also a scrying mirror," Balthazar says. "A tool of divination. Look, Jessamine. Look and tell us what you see."

We join hands. I stare into the watery surface. Light begins to peek through. The edges are vague and shadowy. Before hardly any time has passed, I see Mother sitting by the fire, writing in a small book. Her figure wavers and looks insubstantial, as if she is a ghost. Now I see her asleep, her face still and beautiful. Here she is pouring tea. All these images come and go, lasting only a second or so, like clouds passing over the moon.

And then the scent of Cameo Rose surrounds me. My heart rises. "Mother," I whisper.

Tears are brimming in my eyes. I swallow and continue to concentrate. I see Mother before the fire again, drinking absinthe. She looks tired. For a moment I think I hear the word "Jessamine," but it is faint, as if called from far, far away.

A shadow appears at the edge of the scene. Mother looks up from the fire, wary, as if she has taken note. I see something. A shadow is moving, slithering along the floor.

Mother stands up. Her eyes widen. The picture is shrinking in on itself, growing smaller, a circle closing in until I can see nothing.

And then I hear a voice.

"Beyond the grave I come."

Mother screams.

"No!" I shout, opening my eyes and breaking the circle. "Mother!"

Emily takes my hand again and squeezes it.

"I saw her," I tell them. "Mother. At home. And I heard a voice."

"A voice?" Balthazar asks.

I swallow, for I don't want to repeat the words, but they come out anyway. "'B-beyond—'" I stutter. "'Beyond the grave I come.'"

The room goes still. Balthazar's face is tense. Gabriel blanches.

"Jess," Balthazar says, leaning in and lowering his voice. "I want you to try again. I know it is difficult, but think on the word 'Mephisto.' Think on this word, and tell us what you see."

I breathe out, exhausted. I feel as if I can go no further. *Beyond the grave I come.* They are terrible words, and I want them out of my head, but it is too late. I have opened myself up to this. *Oh, Mother!*

Balthazar places his hand over mine. "We have to, Jess. We must find and stop them before they grow stronger."

I sniffle, nod once, and look back at the board. I take another calming breath. Emily squeezes my hand tighter. "You can do it, Jess," she says. "Your mum would want you to."

I look at her and smile weakly. "You're right, Em," I say, and extend my other hand to join Gabriel's once more. I look back to the board, now as clear and cool as a gray winter's day. I don't have much to go on, so I recall the words that started this journey: *Ring around the rosy.* I repeat this mantra inside my head for several minutes until I feel as if it will drive me mad. The curls at the back of my neck bristle. The room suddenly feels colder.

I break our circle again and reach for the planchette. "I can feel something," I say, and it is true—thoughts and whispering words in the back of my mind, trying to break through.

Balthazar quickly rises and returns with parchment and ink. "Go ahead, Jessamine," he says. "Let the spirit board guide you."

I place the planchette in the center of the board and lay my fingers upon it. For a moment nothing happens, but then the mist clears and I see letters and symbols again. It is remarkable. My hands zigzag quickly, as they did the first time, when I found the words Balthazar was thinking. A sense of dread settles over me as the planchette moves left, right, up and down. I feel a frightful rush of cold air—the dark and dampness of something under the earth. There is a smell, too —a sharp, putrid odor from which I want to escape.

Two pinpoints of red blaze in my mind's eye.

I gasp, drawing my hands away from the planchette.

"What is it?" Emily asks.

"It was cold and damp," I quietly answer. "I felt something dark. Something evil."

Balthazar peers at the parchment in front of him. He cocks his head and then turns it around so I can see what is written. "Chislehurst . . . *Caves?*" I whisper.

"Yes," he replies. "Curious. Most curious. There are caves under London, Jessamine. Chislehurst is one such place."

"Caves?" Emily asks in astonishment. "In London? With bogeys?"

"Outside of London, Emily," Balthazar replies. "They are old mines, now long out of use."

"Some believe they were built by the druids," Gabriel says, "thousand of years ago."

There is a pause.

"What else did you feel?" Balthazar asks. "You came out of the trance quickly, as if you saw something that unsettled you."

His gaze is intense. *For I will always be watching.*

"I saw two pinpoints of red in a field of black. That's all it was, but I felt a terrible sense of unease."

He nods, taking in my words.

"We must go to these caves," Gabriel suggests, looking at me. "We must seek Mephisto out."

"This is our first true lead," Balthazar agrees. "And after Cora's death, we cannot take anything lightly."

Just hearing him speak of Mother makes me want to weep.

Balthazar looks at me, then at Emily and Gabriel. He stands up and seems to grow even taller in the dark room. "Jess, you'll need your weapons."

I pull the case from the leather satchel. The instruments lie in their bed of red velvet, waiting for their power to be unleashed. I draw out the lash. The handle is braided leather. The five trailing thongs feel weighted at the bottom, as if filled with stone or some other deadly embellishment. I saw what it did to the dressmaker's form. *But what would it do to a monster?* I grip the handle and, releasing a breath, lash out, just as Mother did.

A deafening *crack* rings through the room. I set the lash down and pick up the compass. Now I can see how beautiful it really is. A fine filigree pattern runs along the two legs, which taper into points so sharp, I dare not touch them. I set it back down. Mother's words come back to me:

To most people, these are just simple objects, but to those with supernatural abilities, they are deadly weapons.

Inside the satchel is a leather strap with two buttonholes at either end. I find the pegs on the satchel and push them through. There is a length of extra strap, like a belt that is too long, but by adjusting and fiddling, I somehow find a way to sling it over my shoulder, where it bounces against my hipbone. It feels right, as if it has been waiting for me. My proper English side notices that the leather is a complement to my brown boots, which Darby has cleaned to a fine sheen. But now is not the time for frivolous thoughts.

A malevolent force that lived in darkness and fed on fear. They are necromancers.

We take the South Eastern Railway from Charing Cross to the town of Chislehurst, which lies to the southeast. I wonder what the other passengers think of our little band of travelers: A father with his children? A headmaster with some of his pupils? If only they knew the truth.

We are the League of Ravens, and we are seeking evil where it sleeps.

We arrive at Chiselhurst Station at dusk. It is nothing more than a small depot with a signal box. A few malnourished cats and dogs slink about the place. A sign above a small booth reads STATIONMASTER, but there is no one to be seen.

Balthazar leads the way. "It is a village, really," he points out. "A very old one, where the people keep to themselves and shun visitors."

The moon is bright and gives us plenty of light by which to navigate. We are surrounded by open fields and pastures, here and there a small cottage or farmhouse. I smell wood smoke on the air and spy a windmill some distance away, its massive arms creaking in the wind. It's colder here, without the shelter of buildings and houses, and I feel exposed, as if someone could swoop down at any moment and carry me away.

"So where are the caves?" Emily asks.

"Just up ahead," Balthazar answers.

We stop in the middle of the dirt path we are on. Balthazar looks left, then right. "This way," he says.

We make a right turn and come upon a stand of trees as tall as towering giants. Up ahead, a jagged entrance looms like a terrible yawning mouth.

"The cave," Gabriel whispers.

"Yes, Gabriel," Balthazar says. "Be on your guard. Jessamine's vision has led us here, but we do not know what we shall find." He looks at each of us. "Follow me."

The air grows even colder as we approach the entrance. It is wet and damp, like the sea back home. But is it simply weather, or the presence of something more foreboding?

Balthazar sniffs like a foxhound on the hunt. For a moment he says nothing at all, and then, "Light, Emily."

I hear Emily exhale, as soft as a whisper. I turn to see a nimbus of light radiate from the top of her head and then surround her. In an instant, the darkness is flooded with brilliant luminescence.

The light spreads outward from Emily's body like a candle, glowing brightest at the top of her head. Her hair floats away from her face as if she is underwater.

"I take it Emily told you of her gift?" Balthazar asks.

"Yes," I say, still staring. "But I thought it was only—"

"She is a lightbringer," he says proudly. "A very rare elementalist, one who can bend light and heat at her will."

I continue to gaze at her. I hear her father's words from when I looked in on her past: *I seen the fire inside her.* The light seems to surround her and come from within at the same time. It is truly remarkable. She smiles. "Neat, innit?"

"Emily and Gabriel discovered their abilities early on," Balthazar explains. "In time, you, too, will learn to control your gift."

I pull my gaze away from Emily as we head farther into the cave. Balthazar leads the way, with Emily behind him. I come next, with Gabriel taking up the rear.

We are in a winding tunnel, its walls made of a yellow chalky substance. The dirt beneath our feet crunches as if we are walking on small stones and pebbles. It's stuffy and clammy and reminds me of being in the wardrobe at home, which already seems so long ago. Every now and then I hear the *plink, plink, plink* of water dripping from an unseen roof. If not for Emily, we would be surrounded by darkness.

"The ancients mined these caves for lime and rare minerals," Balthazar quietly points out. "It was a different world then, and much harsher."

I wonder about that and think on what it must have been like to live a thousand years ago, without the modern conveniences we have today.

At first, the path is wide enough for the four of us to walk side by side, but it soon narrows to form a crevice.

"We're stuck," Emily says. "We can't get through."

My heart catches, but then Balthazar exhales deeply, turns sideways, and slides in.

"Skinny, that one." Emily snickers.

We hear Balthazar's voice through the crack. "Come in," he calls, his voice echoing. "One at a time. You first, Emily. I need light."

Emily nods and squeezes through. I look at the narrow passage, then let out a breath and shimmy in, the same way Balthazar did. The walls of the crevice close against my ribs, pressing in so strongly, I feel I will be crushed. Gabriel follows me with a quiet grunt.

When we come out on the other side, we are met by walls covered in a black crusty material, as if hot lava has rushed over them. Water trickles through fissures and crevices. I peer up at a forest of ivory-colored spears. At my feet are objects of the same color, but round and blunt, bringing to mind a graveyard of broken teeth. My clothes are filthy. I can feel the cold seeping into my boots.

Gabriel looks up. "Stalactites," he says. "The ones below are stalagmites."

I look up at the long, gleaming daggers and shudder. I pray that one does not fall.

Balthazar leads the way down the passage. There is no sound at all beyond the echo of our footsteps and the drip of water falling from above. There are places on the rock wall that look like ice, slick and shiny. The path veers to the left, and we walk a few more minutes in silence. Just as the quiet is beginning to unsettle me, Balthazar speaks. "Necromancers embrace the dark, for in the night they find their power. They know what humans fear, and use it against them."

I shudder. *Now he tells us this?*

A howl echoes through the cave.

It is not a human voice. It sounds almost like an animal in distress. But before I can ask what it is, the answer is revealed.

Ahead of us, a figure in shredded black garments seems to appear out of thin air. The face is elongated, and the mouth, a black hole of nothing, hangs open in a silent scream.

"A ghoul," Gabriel hisses.

"Your tools," Balthazar whispers. "Open the satchel, Jessamine."

Every instinct I have is telling me to run. There is a monster in front of us. But then I hear Mother's voice in my head: *Within you lies strength yet to be discovered. Like your father . . . and your mother. Never forget that, Jess.*

I reach across my chest to open the satchel, and right at that moment, the creature comes screaming toward us.

I set my stance as Balthazar taught me to, but I trip on one of the stalagmites and fall back. I immediately rise, and the beast is on us in seconds. Balthazar reaches into his waistcoat and whips out two gleaming daggers. A cold blue light ripples along the edge of each blade. He slashes furiously, but the thing moves with lightning speed, bouncing from wall to wall, as if made of something besides human flesh.

A sound like shattering glass rings throughout the cave. My ears feel as if they will burst. *What is it?* I turn my head quickly to see Gabriel, his mouth open wide. It is coming from him. *Is he singing?*

"The lash!" Balthazar cries. With trembling hands, I quickly open the flap to my satchel and withdraw the whip from its case. The monster reaches for Balthazar's throat, but he steps aside and slashes at its face. The stench is unbearable. Two rows of sharp teeth jut from its lower lip.

"Strike!" Balthazar commands me. "Strike now, Jessamine!"

I grasp the braided handle and, without thinking, lash

out, just as Mother did. The weighted tails coil around the creature's neck and then curl tight, like a snake squeezing its prey, as if it has a mind of its own.

The ghoul grasps at its neck, trying to loosen the whip, but then claps its hands against its ears, as if the sound of Gabriel's singing is more painful. All the while, Gabriel's voice is rising in pitch, an aria full of despair. Cracks appear in the walls. Light dances on Emily's fingertips. She rushes forward and rakes the monster's back with her fingernails. "No!" I shout. "Emily!"

She quickly darts away to stand by my side, breathing hard. Her small handprint begins to glow white-hot on the ghoul's back. The monster screams and twists its arms, trying to reach the spot that now blazes a fearsome red. Balthazar lunges in with his blade, slashing at the demon's heart. Though I wonder if it even has one. A note rings in the air —clear and strong. I turn to see Gabriel, golden harp in hand, plucking the strings. His face is set in fierce determination, his eyes as dark as ever.

"Stop!" the demon howls. "You filth! It burns!"

And then it collapses to the floor of the cave, rolling around in pain. The smell of burning hair and something much worse fills the air.

It opens its mouth, a deep chasm of shadow, and a low sound comes from its throat. After a moment, dread creeps down my spine, for it is speaking. "My master," it says, "has something for you. All of you. You will die suffering."

And then it shakes its terrible head and howls again. "Ring around the rosy, a pocketful of posies. Ashes! Ashes! We all fall down!"

How can this thing know that?

"You pitiful beast," Balthazar hisses. "Jessamine. Release this foul spirit."

I look to Balthazar. *What does he mean?*

"The compass!" Emily shouts. "Use the compass, Jess!"

"Draw back your lash first, Jessamine," Balthazar tells me in a much quieter tone.

Fearful, even with Balthazar's instruction, I release the whip. The tails loosen and seem to slither away. I kneel to set it on the ground, then take the silver compass from the case.

"Where?" I ask, standing up.

Balthazar points to a space just below the thing's monstrous feet. "Here," he says. "It is the Circle of Confinement, from which no evil can escape."

I kneel back down and pull the two points of the compass apart. Gabriel is still playing his harp, the notes like darts of pain in the beast's body, for it can now barely move and lies on the floor breathing hard. Its eyes are a sick, vibrant yellow.

Emily stands next to me, her light pulsing in time with my heartbeat.

I put one point of the compass into the rocky earth and slowly turn it in a circle. I gasp. My hands are bathed in a golden glow. Sparks fly up from the ground.

"Now do the same above," Balthazar instructs me. "A creature must be bound at the north and south points. Only then can it be destroyed."

I don't have time to think about it. I just have to do it, so I quickly rise and make a circle at the top of the monster's head. I try to hold my breath, for it emits such a foul odor. Once again, my hands glow as I do my work. The thing's eyes are rolling around like marbles.

"Now the holy water," Balthazar says.

The monster writhes and moans, its body burned by Emily's fire and pierced by Gabriel's notes.

I grasp the vial of holy water and pull out the stopper.

"All it takes is one drop," Balthazar tells me.

I let out a breath and hold the bottle over the circle.

"No!" the ghoul cries.

"*Yes,*" Gabriel hisses, and strikes a melancholy chord.

One drop lands with a *plink*, and the cave is filled with black smoke. I cough, waving my free hand in front of my face. There is another dreadful howl—and then silence.

Sweat pours down my face. Amidst all this madness, I can think of only one thing. It is unseemly for a lady to sweat.

I look down. All that remains of the ghoul is a pool of black ooze.

"Come," Balthazar says, wiping his blades along the rough stone wall. "We must find their lair if we are to—"

He stops and narrows his eyes at something in the distance. I turn around.

Ahead of us, five hooded figures step from the darkness.

Emily's light immediately dims, as if blown out by a foul wind. My legs begin to tremble. Gabriel takes a deep breath, as if he is about to use his voice like a trumpet.

"Wait," whispers Balthazar, extending an arm toward Gabriel. "There are too many."

I peer into the shadows ahead of me, and a voice drifts through the suffocating air. "The child," one of them calls. "Come to us, darkling."

My heart lurches, and I feel as if I will swoon, for the voice is unlike any I have ever heard before—as soft as a woman's and as deep as a man's, combined in an eerie pitch.

"Go back, revenant," Gabriel hisses.

"Come to us, Jessamine," it calls. "Come, darkling."

No, I whisper in my head. *It said my name. No. No. No. No . . .*

"We do not fear the dark!" Balthazar shouts back. "Tell your master that the League of Ravens lives again!"

He raises his hands in front of him and, releasing a heavy breath, claps them together. He closes his eyes. A boom echoes in the cave. I feel it along my spine. The air around me stirs. The earth below my feet feels unsteady. Emily reaches out to the wall to steady herself. Small pebbles and dirt fall from the roof. I am blinded as a flash of light illuminates the cave.

"Follow me!" Balthazar shouts. "Now!

There is no time to think, only to act. My feet move of their own volition, and we race after Balthazar. I leap over the stalagmites, breaking some as I run. Sweat pours down my face. The roof of the cave is falling. My legs are burning. Emily and Gabriel are in front of me, moving with speed I cannot match. Behind me, amidst the din of breaking stone, I hear the strange voice calling me back. "Come to us, Jessamine! Come, darkling!"

CHAPTER FOURTEEN

A Cry in the Night

We are in the parlor. Weak morning sunlight bleeds through the windows. Emily is asleep in a wingback chair across from me, her breath coming in quiet, easy puffs. She didn't even make it up the steps. I can still see her fingers glowing white-hot as she clawed at the devilish creature. Gabriel sits and scribbles in his little book. *He used his voice as a weapon. How?*

I have barely slept. Before I got into bed, I took one last look at my weapons. The braided ends of the lash were still wet with the ghoul's blood. The battle remains a blur. All I can recall is the whip lashing out and then curling around the beast's neck. *To most people these are just simple objects, but to those with supernatural abilities, they are deadly weapons.*

Sleep was troublesome, and although I was exhausted after our ordeal, I tossed and turned before finally falling into a tense slumber. It is not only my body that is drained but my mind and spirit as well. I stare at my hands.

I have killed a ghoul.

A ghoul.

Balthazar strides into the room, bringing me back to the moment. He is wearing cream-colored jodhpurs, a houndstooth jacket, and a white ascot. Black boots rise to his knees. I almost laugh aloud, as if some sort of hysteria has overtaken me. Amidst the madness we have just experienced, I imagine he must be a faerie who likes riding. He takes a seat next to Emily and looks into her sleeping face.

I swallow hard and ask the question that is plaguing me. "'Darkling.' What does that mean? Why did they call me that?"

Balthazar shakes his head slowly, as if he is also perplexed. "I truly do not know, my child. I have never heard such a name before. But it seems as if you are the prey they seek."

Come to us, Jessamine. Come, darkling.

"These creatures have some intelligence guiding them," he continues. "Their reference to a master is troubling, and never before have I heard a ghoul use human speech."

"What were they like before?" I ask.

"Thralls," Balthazar says. "Undead servants with no intelligence, controlled only by the necromancers who raised them."

I try to imagine what kind of person could revel in such unholy evil, but I am confounded. I have so many thoughts, I don't know where to begin. "How did you—what was it? Our escape. The lightning and the breaking stone?"

He sweeps a curl of white hair from Emily's eyes. "My kind are blessed with gifts of spirit and air, which gives us power over the elements, but only for a short while, and only at great cost."

For the first time, I notice how drawn his face is. The spark in his silver eyes is somewhat dimmed.

"There were too many for us to face," he says, almost apologetically. "I had no choice but to destroy the cave. And now we do not know what else lurks within, nor do we have any further information on this 'rosy' business."

Emily stirs and yawns. "Hullo," she says sleepily. She looks exhausted. Dark half-moons shade her eyes.

I stare for a moment before I greet her. "How are you feeling?"

She looks at me blankly, as if I am speaking another language.

Darby enters with tea and scones. She is back to her subservient self, not the smiling girl who was thrilled to receive a new dress. *How much does she know of all this?* She sets the tea service on the table, and her eyes flit to Emily.

"Hullo, wolf girl," Emily greets her.

I almost gasp aloud.

Darby studies the floor.

"Emily," Balthazar says calmly, like a headmaster about to reproach an unruly student, "that is not Darby's name."

Gabriel closes his eyes and sighs.

"It's all right," Darby says, looking back up, but at no one in particular. "I don't mind."

"Can I have some water, please?" Emily asks sweetly.

Darby smiles and leaves the room quietly.

When she is out of hearing distance, I turn to Balthazar. "How much does she know?" I whisper. "About us? About the League of Ravens?"

"Well, she certainly knows that her master is not an ordinary chap," he answers, "and that the children who reside in this house are quite unusual."

"She could join us," I suggest, looking to Gabriel and Emily for support. "We would accept her, and she would be an equal. I think she could use a friend."

"I think so too," Emily says. "She's all right, you know? We could've used a wolf against those monsters."

"Darby cannot change at will," Balthazar says wearily, as if he has stated it before. "Only on the full moon can she make the transformation."

Darby comes back into the room bearing a tray with a ewer of water and glasses. She fills one and hands it to Emily, who gulps it down without pausing.

"Thank you," she says. "I need water after I light up. If I don't drink, it feels like I'm gonna burn to a crisp."

And then she belches.

The color blooms in her cheeks. Darby almost laughs aloud, but quickly turns to leave.

"The rhyme," Gabriel says, looking up from his book. "The one the ghoul spoke. It is the same one we heard from the boy in the alley."

"'Ring around the rosy, a pocketful of posies,'" I whisper.

"How would that thing know that?" Emily asks.

Balthazar turns to her. "That is what we must find out."

The remainder of the day is spent quietly, each of us with our own thoughts. We are waiting for our next move, whatever it may be. I am beyond exhausted. Mother's death, the ghoul in the cave — it is all too much to bear.

But still, after everyone retires I spend a few minutes looking at some of the assorted books piled in the sitting room. *Darkling*, it called me. *What does it mean?*

Most of the tomes I find are of a fantastical nature: *The Black Book of Signs, The Carved Deck, The Land and Its Terrors, A History of the Seelie and Unseelie Court*, but nothing that mentions "darkling."

I hear footsteps, and Emily creeps into the room. I thought she would be sleeping. "Oi," she calls. "What are you doing slinking about?"

"I'm not slinking," I answer. "I'm trying to find out more about this darkling business."

She looks around as if she might find something of interest, but then sits at the table, props her elbows up, and rests her chin in her hands. I join her. I wonder what other evils she has seen, and if fighting ghouls is as disturbing to her as it is to me.

"Was this your first time?" I ask. "Seeing . . . something out of a nightmare?"

"No. I seen something before. It were awful." She looks down at the table and then back up. "It were at Nowhere, right? Olly and Rags said there were a monster in the forest, but we couldn't go out at night, see? But one night me and Gabbyshins snuck out." A mischievous grin forms on her face.

"What did you see?" I ask her. "Did you find anything?"

"Yeah. We found it. We looked all around in the woods, and didn't see nothing. I used my light to show the way. And right when we was headed back, I seen it."

"What? What did you see?"

"A hellhound."

"What is a hellhound?"

"A hound from Hell, innit?"

"I suppose so," I say.

"Well, first it were a man, and then it turned into a dog," Emily clarifies, as if that really helps. "It came after us, me and Gabbyshins. I had to . . . I had to kill it."

Her face looks pained, and I stop the conversation there.

I've already had enough of monsters, and we've only just begun.

When I dream, it is of a long, endless tunnel. A billowing white mist writhes around my body. There is a sound like the screeching of birds, which rings in my ears so shrilly, I cover them with my hands. Somewhere within the darkness, two red flames burn and flicker.

Come to us, Jessamine. I hear the voices call. *Come, darkling.*

Shattering glass jolts me from sleep.

I bolt upright. Sweat dampens my brow. I lie still for another minute, my heart racing. Muffled voices drift through the door. I get up from bed and quickly throw on my nightdress. I take the lash from my satchel.

It could be a ghoul. One who has discovered our location. *My master has something for you. All of you.*

The hallway is dark, and I walk blindly, but the house is so small, I know where each footfall lands. The smell of wood smoke rises in my nostrils, and I wonder who is up this late.

There. Another sound. *Whimpering?* It is coming from

Darby's room. A light glows along the bottom of her door. Without even pausing to think it through, I push it open, my lash gripped tightly in my fist.

Darby thrashes on the bed, violently shaking her head back and forth. The remains of a porcelain ewer lie cracked on the floor. Even in the dim firelight, I can see the wild look in her eyes.

"Jess!" Balthazar shouts. "Leave! Leave now!"

But I do not.

I rush to Darby's bedside. "What happened?"

"Her potion!" he exclaims. "I thought there was more. But it is not enough! I was foolish! Too much on my mind as of late." He swallows, and it is the first time I have seen him truly unnerved. "Take her hand," he urges me. "Try to calm her."

I place my lash on the floor and carefully take Darby's hand. A shiver runs through me. Her nails are as sharp as daggers, and fine brown hair stands out on her forearms. Balthazar is trying to pour the last remaining drops from a brown bottle down her throat. "Drink, dear one," he says, tilting her head back. "Drink and put this menace at bay."

But Darby will have none of that.

She shrieks and howls. She curses. Spittle flies from her mouth. Her eyes meet mine—the pupils are vertical yellow slits, like an animal's, and when I try to find the Darby I know, there is nothing there but pure animal rage. Her teeth look as sharp as Father's razor.

Darby wrenches her hand away from mine and quickly, before I have a chance to draw back, slashes out at my face.

"No!" Balthazar cries.

But it is too late.

I cry out as the pain hits me, sharp and hot. I raise my hand to my cheek.

When I pull it away, it is covered with blood.

CHAPTER FIFTEEN

A Silver Ship

My cry seems to snap Darby back to her true self. She stops thrashing and breathes low and guttural. I am reminded of a trembling rabbit I once saw in the forest, taking shelter from some unknown predator. Her eyes land on Balthazar.

"There," he whispers, stroking Darby's brow. "There, child."

She drinks the last remaining drop of potion.

Balthazar reaches into his jacket and pulls out a cloth. He holds it to my cheek. "Press it firmly, Jess."

I take it and do as he asks. The pain is searing, as if I have been struck by a hot poker from the fireplace. Only then does it truly dawn on me: *I was slashed. By a werewolf.*

Darby looks to me for the briefest moment, as if on the verge of knowing what she has done, and then closes her eyes. In less than a minute, she is breathing deeply. I look on in astonishment as the wolf inside her melts away to reveal the girl I know. The teeth recede, and her nails shrink back in on themselves. The short, stiff bristles around her face disappear, leaving only a frightened child.

A *young girl, lashed to a cross, with flames roaring around her.*

Balthazar turns to me. I am shaking, but try to remain calm. "Am I . . . will I be all right?"

He doesn't speak, only tilts his head and gently takes the cloth from my hand, then sets it in a valise by Darby's bed. Several amber bottles are in there, along with a few cork stoppers. He peers at my face. "A werewolf scratch is not always enough to infect," he says. "Often, a deep wound is the only means of transmission. Or drinking water from the footprint of a wolf in the wild."

He's speaking, but I don't even hear him. I've been scratched. *I've been scratched.*

The floor beneath me spins. My head is heavy. I am swooning. I try to rise, but only fall into darkness.

· · ·

I look at my face in the cloudy mirror glass in the morning. The wound is still fresh, an angry red scratch, but much smaller than what I would have imagined. Balthazar put me to bed after I collapsed. I do not recall this, but it is what he has told me. He gave me a salve to rub on the wound, and I am relieved by its coolness.

I am so tired, I feel as if I could sleep for an eternity.

There is a knock at the door, and Emily and Gabriel both enter.

"Hullo," Emily says. Gabriel only nods and takes a seat on the one small chair in the room. Emily hops onto the bed next to me.

"Old Balthy told us what happened," she says, looking into my face and angling her head to get a better look at the wound. "Being a wolf's not so bad," she suggests. "You can hunt, and sleep for a long time. You can howl." Her eyes widen. "You can be a *mind-reading* wolf!"

Gabriel almost laughs.

I take Emily's hand in mine. "I am not sure what will happen," I tell her. "Balthazar says it usually takes more than a scratch to become infected."

Darby enters the room with clean linens in her hands. She freezes in the doorway. "I'm sorry, miss," she starts. "I'll come ba—"

"No," I tell her. "It's all right. Come in, Darby."

Darby glances at Gabriel and Emily and takes a few steps into the room. "I'm so sorry, miss," she says contritely. "Sir told me what happened. I really didn't mean to. It just comes over me, and I can't help meself!"

She sniffles, and tears begin to roll down her cheeks. "Now I'm going to spoil the linen"—she blurts out—"with these tears!"

"It's all right, Darby," I tell her. "I know you meant me no harm."

Emily rises off the bed and approaches Darby. She takes the linens, lays them at the foot of the bed, then wraps her small arms around Darby's waist. I can see Emily's heat pulsing within her, spreading warmth. Darby's mouth opens in surprise. Her arms stand out at her sides, as if she is unsure what to do with them. Finally she relaxes and returns the hug.

"It'll be aright, wolf girl," Emily says, breaking their embrace. "Jess won't come into your room at night and whip you with her lash. She's nice."

Gabriel shakes his head but cannot hide the small grin that forms on his face.

Darby's face is flushed with heat. She looks to me. "Does it hurt, miss?"

"No," I say. "A fearsome itch, though."

I want to put her at ease, this poor girl with this terrible affliction. I remember the mad look in her eyes when she was her wolf self: the snapping teeth, the nails as sharp as razors.

Darby smiles awkwardly and bends to pick up the linens. "Better be off, then," she says. "Oh." She puts the linens back on the bed. "These are yours, miss. That's why I came in."

"Call me Jess, Darby," I tell her.

Darby takes a breath and smoothes her dress with her hands. She looks at Gabriel and Emily and then back to me. "Okay, miss," she says, and turns to leave.

I can only shake my head.

Once the door is closed, Emily hops back onto the bed. "So," she says. "Let me see your fangs."

I spend most of the day resting, being attended to by Balthazar and the others. Darby brings tea and biscuits, and I find that I am ravenous. *Is this a symptom? Will I start craving human flesh?*

The frivolity of Emily and Gabriel's earlier visit seems to have disappeared. It was a distraction from the reality of what has truly happened. I was scratched, and Balthazar says he is not sure of my fate. *Is this the calm before the storm? Will I awake on the full moon with hair and nails and teeth . . . ?*

In the late afternoon, the door creaks open and Balthazar

peeks his head around the corner. It's odd to see him do this, for he is so often very serious.

"Come in," I call.

He strides into the room like a giant cricket and looks as if he will be dining at a fine restaurant. He is wearing creamy yellow buckskin breeches and a claw-hammer coat that clings to his slender frame. He stands next to me and lays a cool hand on my forehead. "Do you feel feverish?"

"No. Just exhausted, as if I will never regain my strength."

"You have been through much these past few days."

He sits in the small chair, which makes him look absolutely absurd. For a moment, there is nothing but silence, with just the two of us staring at each other. "I am sorry for what has happened, Jess," he finally says. "It is no fault of Darby's, but my own. When she transforms, she is in an entirely different state, torn between the human world and the one that calls to her at night."

"What was that potion?" I ask. "The one you made her drink."

"Wolfsbane," he replies, "also known as *Aconitum lycoctonum*. But it contains herbs and plants from my land as well, something that cannot be found here. I had several doses, but without realizing it, my supply had dwindled. I think your arrival and news of your mother's passing befuddled my mind."

He runs his fingers through his hair.

"Where is your land?" I ask tentatively, sitting up. "When we were returning from Mother's funeral, you said you would tell me more."

Balthazar gazes at me, and his sea-gray eyes flicker. "Some call it the Pleasant Plain," he murmurs. "Others, The Land. But names cannot truly describe its beauty."

"Tell me," I implore. "What does it look like?"

He remains still for a long minute, then—"Look for yourself, child."

At first I don't understand, but then it dawns on me: he wants me to look into his mind.

He closes his eyes. I watch his chest rise and fall, as if he is suddenly fast asleep. I stare at his face—the thin, prominent nose; the high, angled cheekbones. Silken black hair falls like rippling water about his shoulders. I close my eyes and feel the bed beneath me disappear, as if I am floating. The familiar tingle tickles my forehead. I open my eyes. A coil of white, starry mist trails from Balthazar's head to mine. I close my eyes again, and then the images come.

I find myself standing on the endless shore of a vast ocean, with white waves breaking against a cliff face of jagged black rock.

Far in the distance, a mountain looms tall and majestic, its peak wreathed in scarlet clouds. The white sand under my feet is fine, yet I can see each and every grain, sparkling like diamonds. Far away, I hear tinkling bells and am compelled to follow.

I reach down and pick up a handful of sand, then let it fall through my fingers.

The bells are louder now, and another curious sound joins them. It is a song, sung in a clear, high voice, one that I have heard before.

"The smile upon her bonnie cheek
Was sweeter than the bee;
Her voice excelled the birdie's song
Upon the birchen tree."

It is Father's song.

I feel myself drifting, although I am standing still. The tide pools around my bare feet. I look up, out onto the ocean. A small ship with a silver sail rocks on the water. My heart aches.

"Jess," I hear a voice call. "Jessamine."

I open my eyes. Balthazar stands before me. "That is all," he says. "You can go no further."

My head is foggy. "It was beautiful," I whisper.

"Yes. Beautiful beyond words."

"Is that your home?"

"Of a sort. The realm of Faerie is in the mind, as much as it is all around us."

I truly do not understand.

"Tell me more," I demand. "The silver ship. What was it? Where was it going?"

Balthazar smiles, and it is a sad smile. "I cannot show

you more, dear one. For once mere humans glimpse the white shores of Faerie, they often go mad with desire. Let's leave it at that, shall we?" He takes my hand. "Sleep now, Jess. Our work is not yet done."

And then he leaves the room, his boots clicking on the floor.

CHAPTER SIXTEEN

A Message Revealed

The image of the silver ship has stayed with me and brings such a sad, melancholy longing when I think of it. But at the same time, it feels joyful. It is truly a conundrum.

Late this afternoon I find Emily and Gabriel in the parlor playing a game of jackstraws. Dust motes filter through the windows, and a halo of light surrounds Gabriel's head. They look up as I enter.

"You all right, then?" Gabriel asks.

I feel a wave of embarrassment and absently reach up to touch my face. "Y-yes," I stutter. "Much improved." I try to smile, but I am not convinced that it looks genuine. Now that I am feeling better, other thoughts have returned. *Come to us, Jessamine. Come, darkling.*

Gabriel spills the thin sticks onto the floor, creating a toppled forest. Each player must take a turn and remove the sticks one by one. Whoever picks up the most without upsetting the pile wins. I find it troubling that they are playing a childhood game when the world outside is full of ghouls and necromancers.

I walk out and into the back garden. To my surprise, Balthazar is here, sitting on a stone bench. A Roman bust, covered in ivy, lies broken among the high weeds. The air is cold, and I immediately want to rush back inside, but instead I take a seat next to him.

"Ah," he says, distractedly. "How are you feeling?"

"Rather well," I tell him. And it is true. My scratch is now only a faint red line. *A battle scar, just like Jess the Pirate Girl.* I sniffle a little at the memory of that childhood silliness. Now I have seen things that would send a strong man into madness.

Balthazar's gaze seems to drift over my face, not focusing on me. He looks at my hands. *Does he expect them to be as sharp as razors? Covered in hair?*

"Any dreams?" he inquires, raising his head. "Anything . . . unusual?"

"No," I answer, but recall my visions of the white mist

and the terrible sound. "Why do you ask?" I'm growing concerned. "Do you think I'm going to—"

"I just want to be certain," he says mysteriously.

"Certain? Of what?"

He reaches out and touches the scar. I do not draw back, for there is nothing threatening or impolite about it. Right at that moment, Gabriel and Emily appear.

"Having a party and you didn't invite us?" Emily asks.

Neither Balthazar nor I answer.

"Gabbyshins cheats at jackstraws," she complains. "I had to quit." With her elbows, she nudges Gabriel, who only shakes his head.

Emily seems so childlike, but then I remember how she scratched the ghoul's back with her white-hot fingernails, and the thought vanishes.

Balthazar stands up suddenly. "Right, then," he says. "You're all here." He pauses. "I have been called away. There is a matter I must attend to, and it cannot go unbidden."

I am taken aback.

"This I must stress," he says, looking at the three of us. "Do not attempt to reach out to Mephisto on your own. Do you understand?"

Emily gives a sour look. Gabriel is silent. But I will not be. "So we're just supposed to sit here and wait for you? There could be an attack. Who knows what might happen?"

Balthazar kneels by the bench and takes my hand in his.

"Jessamine. I implore you to wait for my return." He says this with an air of authority that I cannot ignore.

"How long will you be gone?" I ask.

"Hopefully only a short while. Two days at most."

"Blimey," Emily mutters.

He stands back up. "Be careful, and always be on your guard. And, again, do not attempt to reach Mephisto without me."

And with that final warning, he turns and walks back inside the house.

I sit in my room, staring at my hands. *How could Balthazar just venture off in the midst of our mission?*

After Mother died, he said we would avenge her. How can we do that when he is not here to guide us? We've done nothing since the attack in the cave.

I glance at my satchel. Those are Father's weapons in there. *"Within you lies strength yet to be discovered,"* Mother told me. *"Like your father . . . and your mother."*

And it is then that I know what I must do.

I draw out the spirit board, and we gather around the table.

"Jessamine," Gabriel says hesitantly, "what are you planning to do with that?" His tone sounds almost fearful.

"I am not sure," I answer. "But we need to find out more

about Mephisto and this 'rosy' business. Balthazar isn't giving us any answers, right?"

They look at each other warily.

"He said to not try anything while he's away," Emily reminds me.

"He's got his own way of doing things," Gabriel says. "He always takes his time."

"He's a faerie," Emily says, as if this is a completely natural explanation. "They take a long time to do *anything*. One time it took him a bloody hour just to answer a question."

I shake my head. "We need answers. The boy in the alley and the ghoul recited the same rhyme. We have to find out more." I take a calming breath and look at both of them. "I don't know what will happen, but I need you here in case something unfortunate occurs. Now, are you with me?"

Emily chews her lip. Gabriel fiddles with his hands. Finally they look at each other and nod at the same time.

I find parchment, quill, and ink and place them on the table. "Write down the words that the planchette spells out, Emily."

"Don't know me letters, Jess."

She says this without the slightest hint of embarrassment. It is I who feel like a beast. I should have known. "Oh—" I start. "I'm sorry. Well, perhaps I can teach you one day."

"Would you, Jess?" Her voice is eager.

"Yes," I tell her.

Gabriel takes the quill in his hand and dips it into the inkwell.

"We need candles," I say, rising, but Emily's small hand stops me short.

"No. I can do that."

I sit back down.

Emily closes her eyes. She breathes out through her nose several times. Little sparks of light flicker around her face and then spread outward, illuminating the table. I can see the spirit board clearly now. She sits back and smiles.

"All right, then," I say, letting out a breath.

I suddenly realize that I have not used the spirit board in quite this manner before. I have never asked it a direct question. *Does it even work that way?*

I place my fingers on the planchette. "'Ring around the rosy,'" I begin. "'A pocketful of posies.' What is the meaning of these words?"

My fingers immediately tingle. The back of my neck goes cold, as if I have stepped out into a winter's day without a scarf. A chill rises in the room. Emily hugs her arms to her chest. Gabriel looks on with a determined gaze. I close my eyes. At first there is only a black curtain, but slowly, like white stars filling a night sky, I see it—a face, as white as alabaster, with raven-black hair falling to either side. The eyes are two red embers. I hold the image in my mind, although it is unsettling. The planchette scrapes across the board—to the left, now right, now down. I swallow and feel sweat on my brow. The face disappears, to be replaced by a tunnel—a long passage filled with white fog. I hear screeching, a terrible grinding sound that sets my nerves on edge.

My hands suddenly stop moving. I take a breath and open my eyes. Emily's light is a warm yellow and spills across the table. I look to Gabriel, whose face is troubled. We do not speak, but he turns the parchment so I can read what is written.

But before I can take in the words—

"Come to me, darkling," a disembodied voice calls out. "Come to me and save your city."

My heart thuds in my chest.

Emily's light goes out.

"Who are you?" I demand, my eyes flitting about the room. "Show yourself!"

A dreadful pause, and then—

"Soon, my lovely. Very soon."

The table begins to vibrate. I lay my hands palms down on the surface, as if somehow I can stop it. The legs begin to shake, drumming the floor beneath me. Gabriel and Emily both stand quickly. "Stop!" I shout, but to whom I do not know. Gabriel reaches into his coat and takes out his harp, but before he can play a calming note, the spirit board rises up and flies across the room.

CHAPTER SEVENTEEN

The Old Nichol

Come to me, darkling. Come to me and save your city.

The words burrow into my brain, and I cannot be rid of them. None of us speak for a long moment.

"Well," Emily finally says, "looks like old Balthy was right."

Her tone makes me bristle. My hands are shaking. "I had to," I say in defense. "I won't stand by doing nothing while my parents' killers are out there."

These words seem to cast even more of a pall over the room.

"There was more," Gabriel finally says. "The words revealed on the spirit board."

He's right, and only now do I recall them, but Gabriel speaks first. "Beyond the grave I come."

My heart aches. "The same as when I had the vision of Mother," I whisper.

I sleep fitfully and remain in my room the next day, only venturing out to join Emily and Gabriel for tea. We all sit with a silent sense of guilt, knowing we have not heeded Balthazar's warning. Even Emily is quiet for once. Darby floats through the halls like a ghost, doing her chores without speaking.

It was all my fault.

Beyond the grave I come.

Balthazar finally returns the next morning without explanation. We tell him what has happened, and his face is grim. He scolds us as if we are schoolchildren. "That was very dangerous, Jess. You could have opened yourself up to attack."

We are in the parlor. Gabriel cradles his harp between his legs, polishing the wood with a cloth, and Emily sits cross-legged before the fire.

Balthazar begins to pace, taking long strides across the

room, his hands behind his back, just as Father used to. "Tell me again," he says, "of this face."

I breathe out and settle my nerves. "It was a cold white face, one whose features I could not really see. But the eyes —they were as red as embers."

Silence falls between us, but for the sound of Balthazar's boots on the floor.

"And the words?" he asks in a tone I do not like.

I swallow and repeat the phrase I cannot forget. "'Come to me, darkling. Come to me and save your city.'" I feel dreadful just saying it aloud. "What do they want with me?" I ask the room.

"Retribution," Balthazar says, his nervous pacing finally coming to a stop. "Remember, Jessamine—your father was instrumental in destroying Mephisto in the past. It is vengeance they seek. First the wife and then the—"

He stops short, as if realizing what he is about to say. He sighs. "They are trying to lure you with threats. Surely it is only a trap."

I think on that a moment. What would Father do? *Always the first to rush into battle,* Balthazar had said.

I feel an ache in my temples, and look down to see that I am gripping the armrest of my chair so tightly my knuckles are white. I've had enough. Everything is bottled up inside me, and now it needs to be released. "But we need to act!" I say firmly.

Emily flinches at my outburst. For a moment I worry that I have spoken out of turn, but then my resolve stiffens. "We have to do *something*. Mephisto is out there right now. It is me they are seeking! The voice said come to me and save your city. If I go to them, I might be able to—"

"No," Balthazar says curtly. "I told you before that they cannot be trusted. I will not allow you to walk blindly into their midst, wherever that may be."

Emily and Gabriel shrink at Balthazar's tone. I try to look into his mind, to see where he has been, but the way is blocked by a dense forest of trees. I could only do it before because he allowed me to, I realize.

"Now," he says, letting out a labored breath and tugging the ends of his waistcoat, as if everything is settled, "there is something I want to show you. Come. Gather your coats."

Before we depart, I make sure to take my weapons.

I am feeling rather on edge as we depart 17 Wadsworth Place. Mother said I have strength yet to be discovered, yet Balthazar is holding me back.

We take an omnibus to a small neighborhood not far from ours. It is called the Old Nichol, Balthazar tells us, and the narrow, winding streets run like a crooked maze throughout. Every terrace house seems to have cracked windows. The smell of fish and sewage rises on the air. I hear a baby's desperate cry from somewhere nearby, and I want to shut my ears to the sound, for it will not stop. I feel an overwhelming sense of sadness.

We arrive at a tenement that is on the verge of collapse. The windows are shattered. I run my finger along the brick, and it comes away black. "A fire?" I ask.

"Soot," Balthazar replies. "From the nearby factory."

I look down. A fine, dark dust peppers my clothes.

"Crikey," Emily says, peering around. "I thought Nowhere was bad."

"This is one of the worst slums in England, Emily," Balthazar says. "People are left to fend for themselves here, with no help or concern from those sworn to protect them."

"It's terrible," I say.

One of the doors has an iron grate in front of it, and Balthazar pulls it away. The whole thing comes off its hinges and falls squeaking and groaning to the ground.

"Follow me," he says. And then—"You may want to cover your noses."

I take out my handkerchief and hold it warily to my face.

The ground-level flat we step into is just one small room. The only light is from a broken window. A sharp, gaseous odor surrounds me, and I wince. I once had the unfortunate experience of detecting such a smell from a dead cat down at the docks. *What will we find here?* I press my handkerchief more firmly. Emily and Gabriel look a little pale, but they only hold their fists to their noses.

"Just in here," Balthazar says.

We step around piles of tin cans and broken bottles, the remains of a small fire. Cracked oil lamps and several pairs of battered shoes are on the floor. There is another door, one I did not see when we entered, and that is where we follow Balthazar. It is here that the smell is the strongest, and now I see its source.

Bodies.

Two bodies are laid out on the rotting floorboards. It is a man and a woman. Their faces are composed, as if sleeping, but it is a sleep from which they will never awaken.

"Bloody hell," Emily mutters.

"How did they die?" I ask through my handkerchief.

Balthazar kneels down and, with one finger, turns the man's head to the side. "Here," he says.

Hesitantly, Emily, Gabriel, and I kneel down too. I look closely at the man's neck, which is mottled with purple bruises. "The rosy sickness?" I venture.

"No," Balthazar says. "Watch."

I look on with morbid fascination. To my horror, Balthazar digs his fingers into the man's neck. I close my eyes in revulsion but open them only to see him pull something out, which makes an awful squelching sound.

He holds it up, and the weak light in the room reveals a curious instrument. It is an iron-gray cylinder, like a small tube, caked with blood. I swallow and try to stay strong, although this entire venture is dreadful beyond belief.

"What in the name of God is that?" I ask.

Balthazar tosses the tube aside. "It is a draining device," he says. "These bodies are completely drained of blood."

Emily stands up and walks closer to the dead woman's body. I peer at her sleeping face. Her long black hair falls to her shoulders, but her skin is sallow and mottled. *Does she have a daughter?* I wonder. *Someone who loved her, the way I loved Mother?*

Emily reaches down and points to the woman's neck. "Same here," she says. "Looks like somebody done sucked the blood right out of 'em. Like they was being had for supper."

I close my eyes.

"Vampire?" Gabriel suggests.

Balthazar stands up. "No, Gabriel. A vampire takes only what is needed to sustain him. There is no blood left in these bodies at all."

"How did you even find this place?" I ask, staring around the ruinous room.

Balthazar takes a handkerchief from within his coat and wipes his hands. "It is easy to find people who will take a few coins to keep their eyes and ears open," he says. "All over the East End, I have heard reports of corpses just like these, drained of every drop of blood."

"Mephisto?" I ask.

"It has to be," Balthazar says. "But to what end?"

We exit the omnibus near the High Street and walk back to 17 Wadsworth Place. The day is gray and cold, and the clouds seem to slowly drift down to earth and swallow us in a heavy fog. The bodies in the Old Nichol are still with me. I will carry their faces forever.

There is noise and commotion everywhere: children running barefoot or begging for scraps of food, men pushing carts full of rubbish, and vendors shouting out their best bargains of the day. Dogs and cats as thin as skeletons root in trash heaps.

A woman leans out of a high tenement window and empties a chamber pot into the street, just barely missing my head. I almost gag as the smell rises up to greet me. I can't imagine what I would have done if it had landed on me.

As we pass a jeweler's shop, a man in dirty clothes blocks our path. Small, piggish eyes dart around in a prunish face. He holds a brush in his hand, and at his feet is a bucket of red paint.

"Excuse us, please, sir," Balthazar says, about to step around him.

The man spits at Balthazar's feet. "It's all your fault! All of you!"

I gasp aloud. Balthazar looks at the spittle and lets out a long, frustrated breath. Emily steps out from behind me. "Piss off!" she shouts.

The man drops his brush, and in the blink of an eye, reaches in his trousers and whips out a crude knife. "Little rat," he hisses.

With one quick movement, Emily kicks out hard with her left foot, catching the man right in his shin. I step back as he crumples to his knees, letting out a string of curses as he does so. The knife falls from his hand and clatters on the cobblestones. Emily scoops it up without missing a beat.

"I think you should be on your way," Balthazar says calmly.

The man picks himself up and stands close to Balthazar, who does not flinch.

"Seen your like before," the man says. "A new day is coming, mark my words." He pauses and narrows his eyes. "You're Irish, eh? I can tell. Hair blacker than coal."

A few people have stopped in the street and are taking in the scene. "Be on your way," Gabriel says fiercely. The man smirks, but something in Gabriel's gaze sends him down the street, leaving his bucket and paintbrush right where we stand. Once he is some distance away, he reaches into his filthy coat, pulls out a bottle, then raises it to his lips, drinking greedily.

"He's touched," Emily says. "What's he on about?"

And that's when I remember.

"He's painting red Xs. Like we saw before, at the clockmaker's."

"What news is this?" Balthazar asks.

We didn't tell him, I realize. It didn't seem important at the time, as all our attention had been focused on the boy in the alley. We quickly fill him in.

"Great calamity!" a voice rings out. "Mysterious sickness strikes London. *Daily Telegraph and Courier.* Great calamity!"

I turn around to see a shabbily dressed newspaper boy shouting at the top of his lungs. Balthazar raises a hand in the air, and the boy approaches. I stare at him. He looks like one of hundreds I've seen in the East End—undernourished, holes in his shoes, and a face that shows the scourge of a hard life.

Balthazar reaches into his coat pocket and gives the boy a shiny coin. His eyes widen. "That's a gold sovereign, sir. That there's a gold sovereign!"

"Keep it, my child," Balthazar tells him.

The newspaper boy swallows, and his tiny Adam's apple bobs up and down. He finally notices Emily, Gabriel, and me and then turns back to Balthazar. "Sir?" he says, looking up at the strange man before him. "Is this a trick, sir?"

Balthazar smiles and plucks a newspaper from the boy's bag. "Be on your way now," he says. "Buy some food for your family."

The boy looks at the coin again. He sniffles. He's going to cry, and I am afraid I will too if he doesn't leave soon. "Bless you, sir," he says, looking up at Balthazar. And then he drops his newspaper sack at his feet and rushes off.

Emily smirks. "Got another one of them there coins?"

Balthazar shakes his head. "Come," he says. "Over here."

We move away from the commotion on the street and huddle under the awning of a bakery. Balthazar snaps open the paper so the front page is revealed. I lean in closer to read:

THE GREAT CALAMITY

TO THE INHABITANTS OF LONDON AND ITS ENVIRONS

It is deemed proper to call attention to Symptoms & Remedies of what has been deemed The Great Calamity.

SYMPTOMS OF THE DISORDER

Giddiness, nervous agitation, slow pulse, cramps in fingers and toes, a moist, blackened tongue, irregular respiration, weeping red sores.

Victims describe a rosy rash prone to itch, which then spreads to the whole body. Some are disguising the malodorous aroma that accompanies the disease by wearing pouches of fresh herbs and posies. Children in Whitechapel and Bethnal Green have taken to repeating a rhyme that describes the illness.

I pause, struck still. *A rhyme that describes the illness.* I look to Balthazar, who arches an eyebrow. I take a breath and continue reading down the page.

The patients' garments should be burned. Those suffering from the disease should be put to bed, wrapped in hot blankets, with poultices applied to the feet and legs to restore their warmth. Twenty to forty drops of laudanum may be employed in a severe case.

Bishop Frederick Wainsthrop says that the sickness is caused by communists, immigrants, and Gypsies. "They are the harbingers of this catastrophe," he has said, "and are surely spreading the disease as quickly as would vermin."

The hateful words stick in my brain . . . *as would vermin.*

A memory comes to me. It is of Deepa, the Indian girl I

befriended back home. She was a foreigner too, and was set upon daily by ruffians—and I did nothing. *Nothing!*

"A rosy rash," I say. "And posies to hide the smell. Like the boy's song."

"And also spoken by the ghoul," Gabriel adds. "And the burning of garments is surely the ashes."

There is a pause.

"And every one of them falling down dead," Balthazar finishes.

Emily nudges me. "What's it say?" she demands. "C'mon, then."

I tell Emily the news we have read. She shakes her head. "So there's blokes going round saying it were foreigners who caused this sickness, eh?"

A knot forms in my stomach. "Yes, Em. People are blaming them for the disease that's going around. It seems even their businesses are being attacked."

"A root of bitterness has grown in people's hearts," Gabriel says solemnly.

"That ain't right," Emily says.

"It's not," Balthazar agrees. "It is surely Mephisto, spreading lies and hatred, trying to divide the city in two."

Come to me and save your city.

The air suddenly becomes cooler, and I wrap my cloak around my shoulders.

We set off on our way again and pass two raven-haired

children selling kindling from a basket. Their skin is olive-colored. *Will they be set upon too?*

The clip-clop of hooves behind us compels me to turn around.

It is a man driving a wagon with a team of mules up the High Street. Bells jangle in their harnesses. He pulls the reins and comes to a stop. I watch him step from his seat. I am not sure what I am looking at, for he wears a mask, like a bird's head, and a long black cloak. Gloves rise up his arms. Not any part of his skin is showing. The hooked beak is sharp and ivory-colored, and the eyes behind the mask glitter in the grimy yellow light. Even from where I stand several feet away, I can see flies buzzing around the cart. The sound seems to grow in my ears until it is as loud as a swarm of angry bees.

"A plague doctor," Gabriel whispers.

"A what?" Emily asks.

"That's what they called him in ancient times," Gabriel says. "It was the Plague of Justinian, in the sixth century."

Before I can ask how Gabriel knows this, I watch the man shuffle into an alley. He returns a moment later.

And he is dragging a dead body.

Emily gasps.

The corpse has no shoes on its feet and is being pulled along like a rag doll, as if it weighs no more than a few stone. Once the bird man is closer to his cart, he lifts it up and throws it into the back of the wagon, then slaps his hands together and climbs back into his seat. With a flick of the reins, the mules continue down the street.

And the wagon is coming our way.

Gabriel touches my elbow. "Back," he says, but I do not move.

I shudder as it draws closer.

"Jess!" Balthazar shouts.

A blast of foul air rushes up my nostrils. I don't want to look, but it is too late. I have already seen what is within.

More bodies.

A jumbled pile of bodies stuffed into the bed of the cart, and all bearing the same red and purple bruises, like the boy in the alley.

I gag.

Crooked arms and legs stick up at odd angles. Stiff black fingers grasp at the empty air. I feel something vile in the back of my throat. They are all dead. Dead from the sickness.

I look on in horror as a child's hand, dangling from the cart, twitches and then goes still.

Balthazar reaches for my arm to pull me away.

"No!" I tell him. "Wait."

I breathe in and out slowly. A thought comes to me, unbidden. I feel the familiar itch at the center of my forehead, and when I reach up to touch it, red mist swirls from the bird man's head.

Ash and smoke cloud my vision. Overhead, swirling, bruised clouds pulse with lightning. Rats are everywhere, as if the whole of London has been overrun. They skitter on the cobblestones, their long nails scrabbling over the bricks. They speed down alleys and even climb walls. I feel something stir around my feet. A creeping fog slides along the ground and wreathes around my ankles. I hold my breath. If I breathe it in, I know I will die. I just know it.

My face grows warm. Out of the fog comes another face, not the bird man's, but something . . . unknown. It is a cold white face, framed by locks of dark hair. The eyes are two pinpoints of red, and they blaze with an unnatural light. I hear raspy breathing and then: "Come to me, darkling. Come to me, Jessamine."

"No!" I shout, clamping my hands over my ears. "No! No! No!"

"Jess!"

It is Emily, grasping my shoulders. "Wake up, Jess!"

I desperately come to and peer around. My breath is short, and I loosen my scarf, for I feel as if I will suffocate.

"What did you see?" asks Balthazar.

"London," I say breathlessly. "With rats. Everywhere."

"And what else?"

"The same voice. The one in the cave. 'Darkling,' it called." My heart begins to race, beating so fast, I feel as if it will jump out of my chest. "I saw the man with flames for eyes! He was calling me! No! No!"

I crumple into Balthazar's arms.

A note rings in the air. It is pure and bright and surrounds me with peace. I close my eyes. The filth of the city is washed away for a moment. I feel as if I am lying in a bed of lavender. A cool breeze caresses my cheek. My breath steadies. Another note chimes, and I open my eyes.

Gabriel slides his small harp back into his coat.

I ease away from Balthazar to look at Gabriel. "Thank you," I tell him.

"Come," Balthazar says. "We must get Jessamine home."

Balthazar takes my arm as we head back to 17 Wadsworth Place. All my energy is spent, and I lean on him for support.

As we walk, we find to our horror that more red Xs have appeared, scrawled on wooden doors and shop windows.

The dripping red paint makes me think of blood.

CHAPTER EIGHTEEN

Night of Breaking Glass

Balthazar opens the door to 17 Wadsworth Place.

"Blimey," Emily whispers.

The whole front room has been torn apart. Broken furniture has been tossed about, books are shredded and scattered on the floor, and, most frightening of all, long claw marks have ripped through the drab wallpaper. There is a smell in the air like sulfur.

I think back to my encounter with the spirit board. *Soon, my lovely,* the voice had taunted me. *Very soon.*

This is all my fault. They are coming for me.

Balthazar steps farther into the room and surveys the wreckage.

It is then that it hits me.

"Darby!" I shout.

I rush up the steps, gathering my skirts, almost tripping as I do so. I push open the door to her room. "Darby!" I cry, whipping my head from left to right. And then I see it, on the wall behind her bed: a lone letter, written in blood:

M

"I am going to find her," I tell Balthazar, adjusting my satchel over my shoulder. "Mephisto killed my mother and father, and now they have taken Darby. I will not wait any longer!"

Balthazar stands amidst the rubble of the front room and looks around, as if seeing it for the first time. "For all I have done for her, I could not keep her safe," he says absently.

"We have to get her back," Emily says.

"They know our location," Gabriel adds. "It's only a matter of time until they come again."

Heat rises in my cheeks. "I swore an oath to use my power for the good of the land and to strike down evil at any cost."

Emily smiles. Gabriel's lips are set in determination.

"And that's what I'm going to do," I continue. "We are the League of Ravens. And now is our time."

Balthazar comes out of his stupor and looks at the three of us. His face is long. "I am afraid I have let you all down," he says contritely. "I once told you it was time for a new generation to stop the evil that is stirring in the shadows. That day has now come."

"What are you implying?" I ask, curious.

"I have been too cautious," he answers. "Waiting for the clues to fall into place. All the while, Mephisto has been growing stronger."

He seems lost in his thoughts again, his eyes distant. He turns to me. "Go now, Jessamine. Go now and find Darby and avenge your parents."

"You're not coming with us?" Emily asks.

Balthazar lays a hand on her small shoulder. "As Jess said, *you* are the League of Ravens. Your time to strike is now."

"But what will you do?" I ask. "Surely you're not staying here?"

The distracted look returns, along with a wrinkling of the brow and a tightening of his lips. "I have something that I must do greater than this moment—and I cannot let it go unattended."

Unbelievable.

I open my mouth and then close it. I feel like grasping him by the shoulders and shaking him. *What could be more important than finding Darby and stopping Mephisto?*

"I promise to see you again," he says. "And I know you will prevail. All of you."

I do not understand, and I can think of nothing to say. Gabriel and Emily look to me as if I am now their leader. "The spirit board," I suggest. "Maybe there is a clue that can lead us to Mephisto's lair."

I glance about the room.

Emily points behind me. "You mean that?" she asks.

I turn around to see the remains of the spirit board, broken into jagged pieces and lying amidst shards of glass.

Balthazar reaches into his waistcoat pocket, where a gentleman would usually keep a watch, and pulls something out by a length of chain. It is a rock of some sort, with no distinctive color, but I see light reflected in its form.

"This is a faerie stone," he says, and comes to stand in front of me. He loops the chain around my neck. "It is used to guide travelers in unknown realms."

I raise my hand to caress it. It is smooth to the touch.

"I was going to give it to you soon," he says, "when the time was right—but there couldn't be a better occasion than now."

My fingers run along the length of chain.

"Press it firmly," he tells me, "and think on the place or object you want to reach."

I close my eyes and squeeze the stone. For several

seconds there is nothing, but slowly, like a fire being kindled, warmth trickles into my palm. I open my eyes. The stone is flickering with color—sea blue and sunshine yellow, fiery red and deep green. *Mephisto*, I think. *Where are they? How do I find them?*

Cold seeps into my hand. The stone goes black, pulsing with a tiny red light. *Mephisto*, I think again. *Where do they hide?*

A tunnel is before me, a long, winding tube of black. White mist clouds my vision. The grinding, screeching sound rings in my ears again.

I open my eyes. It is the same thing as before, but what does it mean? "Come," I say to Emily and Gabriel, adjusting my satchel. "It's time to find Darby."

Balthazar lays a hand on my cheek. He looks at me for a long moment. "When you find them, Jessamine, show no mercy."

And I promise myself—I will not.

Night has fallen.

The smell of death drifts through the roads and alleys like a poisonous fog.

We start on the High Street, looking for clues. We dart down twisting alleys, explore ruined houses, and even venture into the small forest beyond the edge of the city. The whole time, I see things that make me shudder: sick, weeping children; trash heaps buzzing with flies; and everywhere the diseased, clinging to whatever life they have left.

Jangling bells make me pause. Up ahead, I see the bird man again, trundling down the foggy road with his cart of the dead. He stops at the door of a crumbling house and collects a body shrouded in bedsheets.

"It's him again." Emily says. "The plague doctor."

I looked into his mind before. Maybe I can find a clue—

The sound of breaking glass shatters my thoughts.

I whip my head around. A flaming bottle has been tossed through a shop window, and now the flames rise inside. A mob is forming behind us—men with sticks and makeshift clubs, and one who holds a cutlass, a long, skinny sword that gleams in the night.

"Bloody 'ell," Emily mutters.

Several figures huddle around a shabbily dressed man standing on a wooden crate, bellowing at the top of his lungs. I recoil in horror. It is the same vagabond who spit at us earlier.

"And who's behind this 'ere sickness?" he shouts.

"The Jews!" a voice cries out.

"Gypsies!" yells another.

Spittle flies from the man's mouth. He is enraged. "I say we don't need their kind round here!" he hisses, and the crowd roars back in agreement.

"Foreigners out of our England!" calls a woman's sharp voice.

It's the meeting. The Great Public Meeting called for on the handbill, I realize.

Another flaming bottle crashes through a window.

The fire in the shop is spreading quickly, licking along a length of drapes and rising to the ceiling. "The whole place will be up in flames any minute!" Gabriel shouts.

"C'mon," I urge them, grabbing Emily's arm. "We have to get away from here!"

Now, up and down the street, men and women and even some children smash windows and light fires. Clouds of black smoke plume in the air.

The crowd is growing, and quickly. They overturn carts and wheelbarrows. They scream and shout, grabbing anyone they believe to be a foreigner. I gasp as a man in simple dark clothes is knocked down in the street. His tall hat falls off his head and into the mud. Long curls hang on either side of his face. A large book drops from his hands. "Please!" he cries. "No!"

A man with a club looms over him. I know what he is about to do, but I cannot stop him. *He's too big!* Then I remember Deepa, my friend back home. I didn't help her, but I won't stand by idly now. He raises his club. "It's wrong!" I shout. "Stop!"

The man turns. I reach for my lash. He is the size of a

giant from a storybook. A bloody apron is tied around his waist. He leers at us, revealing broken teeth. "Little buggers!" he hisses.

"Run!" Gabriel cries.

We dash away—to where, I do not know, but away from the madness and rioting—crashing through vendors' carts and crowds of shrieking people. An old woman with a terrible gash across her forehead is moaning in the street, her parcels scattered around her. I can't stop to help her. I can't. We have to keep running. A little farther on, a Gypsy caravan is aflame, the smoke so thick, it almost chokes my throat.

Finally, when I feel as if my legs are about to give out, we stop and rest. We are still on the High Street, but away from the terrible commotion. Gaslights sputter and hiss, providing a soft yellow glow. I hear the shriek of a horse as it gallops by, broken free from its carriage.

We huddle together, winded, hands on knees, catching our breath. I straighten up and peer around. I see no sign of the man in the bloody apron. We are standing in the street amidst a work site. A crane sits motionless, like a giant insect. Mounds of earth have been dug up, and steel beams lie in the trenches, forming tracks.

I realize we are in the same place that we passed when Balthazar led Mother and me to 17 Wadsworth Place. *They call it the Underground,* he had said. *Steam-powered locomotives that will ferry passengers all about London.* An arched brick opening is farther ahead of us. Darkness beckons from within.

"What is it?" Gabriel asks.

I don't answer immediately but look at the newly laid tracks that lead to the ominous entrance. I step closer, nimbly maneuvering around the piles of broken wood, debris, and dirt.

"Wouldn't step any farther, miss," a voice calls out.

I spin around, my hands reaching for my weapons. Emily and Gabriel tense, alert and ready to spring into action.

It is a man, wearing grubby clothes. He stares at us.

"Where does this tunnel lead?" I ask.

He takes off his cap and wrings it in his hands, as if embarrassed. I imagine he believes he is talking to someone from the upper class and should not rise above his station. He looks at Gabriel and Emily and nods politely.

"Well, miss," he starts, "sir. This here tunnel runs from Paddington to Farringdon Street. Quite a marvel, if I may say so myself." He tries to smile, but it comes across all wrong. "No place for a lass, though, begging your pardon."

"What are you doing here?" Gabriel asks. "What is your business?"

The man rubs his hands together. "Well, little sir, I'm just the rag-and-bone man, ain't I? Collecting stuff. Sometimes the workers—the navvies, you know—leave bits and bobs about. Stuff I can sell, see?"

Only now do I see the bag at his feet. He bends down and loosens the drawstring and pulls out several coins. "Found these when they dug up the earth." They clink in his hand.

"Let's go," Emily says. "He's harmless as an old goat."

There is a hissing sound, as if air is being released from a valve. It is coming from within the tunnel.

"Miss?" the man says. "Anything else you be needing?"

"No," I tell him. "Thank you."

He gives a little bow, places his cap back on his head, and ambles away. I continue to stare ahead, into the darkness.

"Jess?" Emily asks warily. "What you thinkin'?"

I squeeze the faerie stone, which glows with white light. "In there," I say, pointing. "We need to go into the Underground."

CHAPTER NINETEEN

Blood Will Out

The air in here is even colder than outside. Without the gaslights, we are in complete darkness.

"What's in here?" Gabriel asks, his voice echoing.

"Darby," I tell him. "And those who took her."

"How do you know?" Emily asks.

"I keep seeing it," I tell them. "In my visions. A tunnel. And there is a screeching sound that feels as if it will split my ears."

"The dreams of a mesmerist are not to be ignored," Gabriel offers.

"Good," I say. "Follow me."

The farther in we walk, the colder it gets. I am reminded of our trip to Chislehurst Caves. Finally, when I can no longer see my hand in front of my face, light flares at the edge of my vision. I turn around.

Emily is emitting a warm glow behind me, illuminating the tunnel. Though I have seen this before, it is still remarkable, this gift of hers. She gives me a small grin.

I look up. The ceiling is crossed with struts and curves, like the ribs of a giant animal. There is no night sky, nor moon or stars, only black. A metal sign on the wall reads NO EXIT in big red letters.

I lead the way, with Emily behind me and Gabriel in the rear. Emily's light spreads out before us, revealing rows of white tiles that line the walls.

I squeeze the faerie stone again, trying to get some sense of where Darby is, but this time, nothing is revealed within its depths. I turn around to see how far we have come, but the entrance has disappeared from sight.

I continue on. We are walking over steel ties, which are spaced a few feet apart. Between them are gravel and stones.

I think of how Mephisto is behind all of this — the rioting and disturbance. It is dreadful. The East End will be torn apart. A sense of suspicion suddenly settles over me. It grows even colder, and the hair on the back of my neck bristles. "Do you feel that?" I ask, my voice bouncing off the walls.

"Cold, innit?" Emily says.

"I feel it too," Gabriel confirms.

"Something is at work here," I say. "Some devilry." I look ahead, keeping my senses alert.

We walk a little farther, and then I see it.

A few feet in front of us, a pale white face rises out of the shadows as if lit by an unseen moon. A tremor runs through my body. Emily and Gabriel gasp. I reach for the flap of my satchel and take out the lash.

It is a ghoul. Shredded rags hang about its body, and the stench of the grave flows in front of it. The eyes glow with malice. It crosses the distance between us in less than a second. Gabriel cries out a stream of words, and the creature flies back as if struck by a great wind. Black smoke wreathes around its head. It quickly lifts itself up and lunges again. I strike out with the lash, tangling it by the feet. Gabriel's voice is rising. It sounds like bells . . . bells from a church tower. "No!" the ghoul screams. "Stop!"

The bells are all around me now, a solemn tolling, one that vibrates in the back of my skull and down my spine.

The fiend slashes out at me with a long arm. I am caught off guard, distracted by the ominous tolling and the creature's long claw slashes my dress.

I raise the lash above my head, and my wrist instinctively twirls, getting ready to strike.

CRACK!

The lash coils around the ghoul's neck and squeezes tight. It falls to its knees, struggling, choking for breath. Emily rushes in and places both hands on either side of the undead creature's face. I can see the light pulsing within her, glowing brighter than ever before. "Die!" she screams.

"Emily!" Gabriel cries. "That's enough!"

But Emily doesn't listen.

"Die!" she screams again.

"Emily!" I shout.

Finally she pulls her hands away, breathing hard. The ghoul's face is burned black. It moans and writhes on the ground. Gabriel takes out his little book and recites words in a language I have never heard before.

"Stop!" the undead creature hisses. "It hurts! Please!"

Gabriel is whispering now, almost as if he is praying. Quickly, I take out the compass and kneel to draw the Circle of Confinement at both points. My hands are bathed in golden light again. I set the compass down, remove the vial of holy water, and hold it over the circle.

"No!" the ghoul screams. "My master wants you! I only come to do his bidding."

For a moment I hesitate. Balthazar said he had never

heard of ghouls speaking. Maybe there is hope for this thing. Maybe it can be saved.

"Jess," Gabriel says.

I turn away from the vile creature and look to him. He doesn't have to say anything, for his thoughts are revealed in his eyes: there is no salvation for this unholy spirit. I know what I must do. What I *have* to do: strike down evil at any cost.

A bead of holy water trembles on the lip of the vial. Time seems to slow down for a second, until I tip the vial into the circle.

The ghoul howls and begins to dissolve before my eyes. It is shrinking in on itself, pooling and bubbling in clouds of black smoke. I stand up and back away. The doomed creature screams once more, and then there is silence.

"Come," I say, undaunted. "Darby must be near."

We head deeper into the tunnel. I look around warily, prepared to face another threat. Emily's light is weaker now, her face somewhat ashen.

"Are you going to be all right?" I ask.

"Yes," she says. "Just need to get me strength back." She swallows. She needs water, I remember. *I need water after I light up. If I don't drink, it feels like I'm gonna burn to a crisp.*

We have no water, and I curse myself for not thinking of it. I am fatigued as well, and my breath feels short. My limbs are sore and burning. A sharp pain in my side makes me wince. I place my hand near my stomach, and it comes away wet. *The ghoul's claw.*

Emily sees the blood on my hands. "You're hurt!" she cries.

They both huddle around, and Emily stands in front of me and lifts the slashed cloth. "Doesn't look too bad," she says.

It might not look bad, I think, *but it certainly hurts.*

"Eat one of the leaves," Gabriel suggests.

For a moment I don't know what he means, until Mother's words echo in my head. *If you ever find yourself hurt, eat one of the leaves.*

I open the satchel. The acacia branch looks alive, as if it is still in bloom. I pluck off one of the leaves and hold it up to Emily's dim light. I place it on my tongue. It dissolves almost instantly.

"How is it, then?" Emily asks.

I lick my lips and try to discern the flavor. "Well. It's sweet. No—it's tart."

Actually, I'm not quite sure how to describe it, but after a moment, warmth spreads in my belly like a spot of sunshine and I immediately feel more at ease.

"Let me try it," Emily says.

She draws a little closer, and I pluck off another leaf.

Emily takes it with her small fingers and pops it into her mouth without hesitation. She nods her head, as if thinking, and then swallows. "Better than mush," she says to Gabriel.

"Gabriel?" I offer, holding out the branch. Maybe he could use some renewed strength too, after our fight.

"No," he says. "Thank you, Jess. I have all the power I need within me."

Strange, I think, and put the branch back into my satchel.

We walk a little more slowly, and I gather my thoughts. It all happened so quickly. The ghoul, Gabriel, the singing and the bells. "I need to know," I say to Gabriel, turning around. "I need to know what else you are gifted with. It's more than just your harp and voice. Tell me, Gabriel. What are you?"

I wait for what seems an eternity. "I promise to tell you," he finally answers. "When all this is over."

"I will hold you to it."

"You will have your answers."

I clutch my lash more tightly and head farther in.

We are now walking three abreast instead of single file, with Emily in the middle. I try to focus on Darby again, or Mephisto—I don't even know which, as my thoughts are jumbled. We walk for several minutes in silence, until Gabriel finally speaks. "They are damned, Jess. They cannot be saved."

"I know," I tell him. "It's just . . . it's sad, isn't it? These creatures—brought back from the dead. Do they even know who they are? *What* they are?"

"There is no place for the dead in the land of the living," Gabriel says thickly.

I step into something wet, as if I am suddenly walking through muck. At the edges of Emily's light I can see a slick pool of liquid, spilling across the tracks. "There's something here," I say, kneeling down.

I take a breath and dip my finger to the ground, but somehow, I already know what it is. "Blood," I whisper.

Searing heat blazes into my forehead.

I am in a dimly lit hall, with an endless row of doors along each side. I sense pain coming from behind each one of them, and screams—oh, so many screams. A ghostly red light pulses around one, and I walk toward it. I turn the handle and slowly step inside.

Something soft and squishy presses against the bottom of my shoe. I look down. It is a dead rat.

I look up. I am not in another room, but in a forest at night. Creaking branches stir in the slight wind. A crescent moon hangs in the sky, providing a soft, glowing light. I can actually feel the cold air on my skin.

I reach out to touch the tree that is in front of me. The bark is rough and sticky, and sap runs in rivulets along its trunk.

My ears perk up to murmuring voices. I step away and look into the forest.

Under a canopy of tall trees, six hooded figures form a circle.

The circle breaks, and I see what they are surrounding.

It is a man.

He is lying on a slab of stone, and he looks dead, for his bare chest does not rise and fall. His eyes are closed, and his skin is as white as ivory. His face is fair to look upon, with a lock of dark hair falling across his forehead and trailing down to a strong nose and chin.

"Master," one of the hooded figures speaks. "As your will commands, we gather to bring you back to this mortal world."

The figure begins an incantation of sorts, guttural and harsh. They are words I have never heard before, and they leave me with a dreadful sense of unease.

He pauses, and the wind whistles through the branches. "Now we begin," he says, and reaches into the folds of his black garments. He pulls out a blade and holds it up with two hands, as if presenting the Holy Grail itself. "The Eternity Blade," he announces. The hilt is encrusted with rubies and gemstones winking in the moonlight. He draws back one of his sleeves and, to my horror, runs the blade along his wrist. He passes the dagger to the next man, who does the same. And then the next, and the next . . .

My blood runs cold at the sight.

One of the men steps forward. He is holding a golden chalice, and with it, he collects drops of blood from each man. When they are finished, the first hooded figure takes the chalice and carries it to the motionless figure on the slab of stone. He holds it up to the closed lips. "Drink, Master," *he says.* "Drink and be reborn."

"Drink and be reborn," *the others echo.*

Cradling the dead man's head in one hand, the leader drips blood into his mouth. "Rise, Malachai," *he says.* "Rise and be reborn."

I hear an inhalation of breath, and the dead man's chest expands. He is breathing. The dead man is breathing. His acolytes gasp and fall to their knees as the man named Malachai rises from the slab.

"Jess, wake up! Come back!"

Emily's voice snaps me awake. I am lying on the ground, with Emily and Gabriel kneeling close. My clothes are soiled with blood and dirt. Emily strokes my hair, which is damp with sweat. "Your eyes rolled back in your head, Jess. You had a fit."

I stand up, and they rise with me. My thoughts are racing. *I touched the blood and then—that name. Malachai.*

It is familiar, but from where? Then I remember Mother's words: *And before your father died, he killed one of the greatest necromancers of all.*

"Jess?" Emily says. "What is it? What did you see?"

"My father's killer," I tell her. "He is alive."

CHAPTER TWENTY

A Warm Embrace

H e was brought back from the dead," I say. "Malachai Grimstead."

"You saw this?" Gabriel asks in astonishment.

"Yes. I saw it all. A cruel blade, cloaked and hooded men. They called him Malachai."

"Black sorcery," Gabriel hisses.

My head feels light, as if I am about to swoon. "He had the same face I saw when we used the spirit board when Balthazar was away—cold and white . . . with red eyes."

Rise, Malachai. Rise and be reborn.

"Jess?" Emily says quietly. "You don't think that was Malachai's blood you touched, do you?"

"I don't know what to think, Emily."

But it is then that I notice a feeling of clarity, a clear, bright spot in my head, like a compass pointing the way. I touch the faerie stone. It is warm, and when I look down, I see that it is glowing red.

"It's trying to tell you something," Emily says.

"It is, Emily, and we have no choice but to go forward."

I take a moment to look at the two of them. They have followed me into uncertain danger, based on what? *My feelings? My visions?* "I'm glad you're with me," I tell them. "I'm glad you're my friends."

"Of course we are," Emily says.

"We know a thing or two about sticking together," Gabriel says, which is the most casually I've ever heard him speak. I imagine he is referring to the orphanage—Nowhere.

"Plus, we've got to revenge your mum and dad," Emily adds.

My eyes water at Emily's words, but I set my shoulders and let out a breath. "Let's be about it, then, shall we?"

Emily and Gabriel fall in behind me, and we press forward.

The darkness looms like a living thing, dense and suffocating. Emily's light is dim. We must find water for her soon.

I hear her small footsteps behind me, soft and light, but her breathing is labored.

I can't get the image out of my head—the dead man on the slab. *Rise, Malachai. Rise and be reborn.*

"*Jessamine.*"

The voice is as soft as a whisper, and it tickles my ear. "Did you hear that?"

"What?" Emily and Gabriel ask at the same time.

"Someone called my name. Listen."

We stand still, silent. My heart beats so loudly, I feel it in my ears.

"*Jessamine.*"

We all turn around at the same time. I look left and right, searching. Emily doesn't speak, but points straight ahead.

At first all I see is a glowing shape, shimmering and surrounded by silver light. A feeling of peacefulness washes over me. It is a woman.

My heart falls to my feet.

No. It can't be.

Emily gasps. "That's your mum!"

I do not answer, only stare ahead.

"It could be a trick," Gabriel says, making the sign of the cross. "Some dark sorcery."

The glowing shape becomes more clear. I feel it reaching

out to me. It is nothing but pure love, like the time Gabriel played his harp—a joy that seeps into every pore of my being.

It *is* Mother.

She runs the few short steps and embraces me. I squeeze her tightly, never wanting to let go. The comforting scent of Cameo Rose blooms in my nostrils. And it is then that I am certain. It truly is Mother.

"Mother," I whisper, breaking our embrace. "How? You're . . ." I touch her face.

"Dead?" she says. "Yes, child, I have passed beyond, and I cannot tarry long. You must listen to me, Jess."

Jess.

"There is something you need to know, dear one."

"What is it, Mother? Tell me. Quickly!"

Emily and Gabriel move closer, eager to hear Mother's words.

She steps back, and her eyes—the soft green eyes I know so well—flood to a deep black. "'Ring around the rosy,'" she cries out. "'A pocketful of posies. Ashes! Ashes! We all fall down!'"

And then she screams.

PART THREE
The Mesmerist

CHAPTER TWENTY-ONE

Rats

S hadows leap from the darkness. Mother fades right before my eyes.

I try to strike out, but cold hands grasp my arms, pinning them back so far, I feel as if they will break. My lash drops to the ground. I struggle with all my might, to no avail. All I see are black shapes within a deeper shade of black. And eyes. Glowing red eyes floating in the darkness.

Emily's light flares brighter than ever for one brief moment and then fizzles. She falls to the tunnel floor. "Emily!" I shout.

A calming note rings out. Whatever it is that is holding me loosens its grip for a moment but then squeezes again, pinching my forearms with what feel like hot irons.

Gabriel strums another chord, but just as quickly it sours, fading off into a discordant tone that twangs and vibrates, as if someone is wrenching the strings out of his harp. I hear a grunt and then silence.

My arms are suddenly released. I spin around, striking out at an unseen foe, but my fist swings through empty air.

"Emily?" I call again. "Gabriel. Where are you?" *I cannot see.* I slowly kneel on my hands and knees and scrabble around in the dirt and rocks, trying to find my lash. It is not here. The pain in my side where I was slashed is now burning again.

I shudder. That was not Mother.

It was an illusion cast by Malachai Grimstead.

They can make shadows appear where none exist, and cast illusions that break one's spirit. Balthazar spoke these words upon our first meeting.

He possessed the power of mesmerism as well, Mother had said, *which made him all the more dangerous, for he used his gift to cause pain and suffering.*

"Emily!" I call out. "Gabriel?"

No answer.

I walk with my arms stretched in front of me, in the

direction of what I think is the tunnel wall. If I can feel the tiles, I'll at least know where I am in this darkness. *But where are Emily and Gabriel?*

I want to call out again, but I do not. It could draw more creatures. *Why have I been left alone? What is happening?*

The stone around my neck glows white. A small pool of light spreads around me. I grasp it and feel warmth spread through my body. I sense something—a thought drifting on the dank air.

Come to me, darkling.

My other hand touches the side of the tunnel and, tracing my fingers along the tile, I lower myself to sit, my back against the wall. I squeeze the faerie stone and close my eyes. Cold, prickly sweat rises on my arms and neck. It is the same feeling I had when I heard the voice from the spirit board. *Soon, my lovely. Very soon.* Now those words ring in my head, as if from only a few feet away, a terrible echo that floats through the dank passage. *SOON . . . SOON . . . SOON.*

I try to summon the face of Malachai Grimstead—the dark hair, the burning red eyes.

I breathe in deeply, thinking of the terrible man on the slab—my father's killer. "*Malachai,*" I whisper. "*Malachai Grimstead.*"

And then I feel myself falling.

I see a clean white room with tall arched windows. Long,

golden rays of sunlight spill onto the marble floor. Gleaming metal tables are set with beakers, tubes, and curious medical devices.

And then there are the rats.

They are enclosed in wire cages along the far wall, running to and fro, their nails clicking and scrabbling.

I am an observer again, the same as when I saw Malachai rise from the dead. But this is different. It is more like the images I saw when the spirit board was used as a scrying mirror to learn about Mother's death.

Mother. My heart pangs.

The scene fades before my eyes. It is as if I am looking through a kaleidoscope, a tool I once saw at a shop, which reveals myriad colors when you stare through the lens.

I am back in the room again, but now there is a man here as well.

It is the same man I saw on the slab: the dark hair, the strong chin, a face as white as ivory.

Malachai Grimstead.

He is bending over a table, observing the glittering insides of a corpse. An audience is seated around him. Blood rises up to his elbows. "The human body contains wonders to behold," his voice echoes, although I do not see his lips move. "As doctors, we are blessed with the gifts of life and death. In our hands hangs the balance."

My head spins.

Now I am elsewhere.

I see a man, sitting behind a large wooden desk stacked with books and papers. The brass plaque in front of him reads Dr. Levy. Daylight streams in through the tall windows and glints off a ring on his finger—a six-pointed star. His brow is furrowed.

He is facing another man, who is impeccably dressed. Everything about him is clean and orderly, down to his trimmed fingernails.

"I am sorry, Malachai," the man behind the desk says. "Your . . . experiments have begun to attract attention." He rubs his pale hands together in what seems to be a nervous gesture. "I'm afraid we will have to discontinue your education here."

Malachai fumes. He stands up quickly, scattering papers from the desk. "You call yourself a scientist?" he bellows. "Your mind cannot comprehend the realms in which I delve. My deeds will go down in history!"

The vision passes, like water being sopped up by a sponge. Red splotches burn behind my eyelids.

I feel disconnected from myself, as if I have no physical body here, just my thoughts, floating . . .

A flash of bright light, and I am back in the room with the rats. Blood drops splatter the floor. The shiny beakers from before are smashed. A foul odor burns my nostrils. A boy sits backed into a corner, wearing only his smallclothes. His skinny knees are drawn up to his chest.

I stiffen.

I know that face. It is the boy from the alley! The Rosy Boy. I hear his voice in my head: Help, *he whispered.* Please, help me.

From the edge of my vision, Malachai enters the scene, a squirming rodent gripped firmly in one hand. In the other, a thin syringe gleams, a drop of liquid balanced at its tip. In one quick motion he plunges it into the rat's thick skin. It squirms, trying to break free, but Malachai holds it tightly. After what seems like forever, he drops the syringe on the floor.

Now he approaches the boy, who winces and draws back. Quicker than a striking cobra, Malachai lashes out with his free hand and grabs the boy's left arm.

"This won't hurt," he says in a flat, dead voice. "Just a pinch."

The boy screams as the rat sinks its teeth into his arm.

"Shush," Malachai whispers in feigned sincerity as the rat scampers away. "Quiet now." He cocks his head. "Do you like to sing?"

"I want to go home," the boy sobs. "I want me mum."

"I want me mum," Malachai cruelly mimics, and then leans in close. "I have a song for you."

I shudder, for I know what is coming.

"Ring around the rosy," Malachai sings quietly. "A pocketful of posies. Ashes! Ashes! We all fall down!"

The monster called Malachai raises his head. "I have given you a rosy gift," he taunts. "Run along now, and spread it to your family and those who come to visit."

I awake, gasping, and stare into the darkness.

Rats. The disease is being spread by rats.

And then I hear it again, the dreadful refrain that has tormented me to no end.

Come to me, darkling. Come to me, Jessamine.

CHAPTER TWENTY-TWO

M

Darkness looms in front of me. The faerie stone has dimmed. I sit with my back against the tunnel wall, my knees drawn up to my chest.

Rats.

Malachai is using rats to spread the rosy sickness.

I have to stop him. But how?

Only now do I notice faint light a short distance away, near the tracks. Five candles are planted in the earth. They form a circle, and the flames sputter and hiss in the stuffy air.

Someone has been here.

"Emily?" I call, my voice hoarse. "Gabriel?"

I stand up and step away from the tunnel wall, slowly approaching the mysterious circle of candles. The smoke is thin, but it burns my eyes and scratches my throat.

"Jess," I hear a weak voice call.

"Emily!" I shout, looking left and right.

And then I see them.

There—farther along the tunnel wall, on the opposite side—two figures are slumped. I race to the spot and kneel to cradle Emily's head in my hands. She is pale and feverish, sweating. Her light is back but pulsing slowly, and her lips are dry and cracked. "Water," she croaks. "I need something . . . to drink."

"We don't have any water, Em," I tell her. "I promise I will get you out of here." And I certainly hope I can.

Next to her, Gabriel is sitting against the wall too, his head lolling on his neck. A long red gash is scored across his face, and his harp lies broken beside him. "Gabriel," I start. "Are you hurt?"

His eyes open and close slowly. I no longer have my satchel and can't even give him an acacia leaf.

"Someone is here," he whispers. It seems as if all the strength has left his body. "We saw him."

"Who?" I ask. "Who did you see?"

"That would be me," a calm voice calls.

I turn quickly, back to the circle of candles. A shape, tall and ghostly, walks toward me. It is him, Malachai. I can feel it in every pore of my skin.

I stand up, scanning the ground for my satchel, thinking that somehow it could be here, not taken by the creatures who attacked us, leaving us defenseless for their master's arrival.

The figure draws closer. "Stay away!" I shout, inching back. My fingertips touch the wall behind me.

And then the words I have heard inside my head for so long are truly spoken aloud.

"Come to me, darkling. Come to me, Jessamine."

The bearer of the voice steps into the circle of candles.

He wears not the skin of a monster, but that of a human man. His black waistcoat looks to be made from velvet, and the vest within is stitched with red paisley swirls. He has the appearance of a gentleman, and the silken ascot tucked into his high-collared white shirt is elegantly knotted.

I am struck still. Father's killer is in front of me. My tongue cleaves to the roof of my mouth. My hands are clammy. For all my talk of bravery, I cannot move, cannot even speak. Waves of heat seem to radiate from him, and my face sweats profusely.

He looks at Emily and Gabriel for a long moment, and then his gaze falls back to me. I feel as if he is searching my very soul, but I force myself not to look away. "I must say, Jessamine," he says, "you run with a rather ragged lot."

The sound of my name in his mouth sickens me.

"Where is the other one?" he asks. "That prancing fop? My old friend Balthazar."

Fear roils in my stomach, a twisting knot of pain, but somehow I find the courage to speak. "Where's Darby?" I demand. "What have you done with her?"

He remains in the circle, and I feel the very air around him stir, as if it wants to escape. "You have your father's look about you," he says. "Before his head left his body."

Killed by a creature of the dark. His body rip—

He makes no move to attack, but only studies me, as if I am one of his rats.

I have to concentrate. *What can I do?*

"Do you know why I call you darkling?"

I do not answer.

"In ancient times, a darkling was a child born with a black soul. Like yours, Jessamine. Death is drawn to you— your father, your dear mother." He raises his head higher and thrusts out his chin. "Stand by my side, darkling, and I will show you how to walk beyond death. I can teach you beautiful things. Terrible, beautiful things."

A candle hisses and burns out. Malachai looks down. Only now do I notice that his gentlemanly appearance has a flaw, for his fingernails drip tears of blood, one of which just snuffed out the candle.

I swallow hard.

"I will never follow you," I reply under my breath.

"Did you like my message?" he asks, ignoring my answer.

He raises his left hand and swirls a bloody finger in the air, as if writing on parchment. "The letter *M,* revealed on your spirit board."

"Mephisto," I whisper.

He cocks his head. "I believe it stands for Malachai," he says, "for I have outgrown my former colleagues. Every drop of blood gives me strength over the power of the grave."

My mind races back to the terrible instrument Balthazar pulled from the dead man's neck. *There have been reports of a creeping shadow at night . . . one that leaves only a trail of crimson blood.*

Why?" I ask, and realize that I sound like a small, lost child. "Why are you doing this?"

He is silent for a moment, and then—"I have mastered death, you see. These servants I have made are only the first step. No longer empty vessels, they have the gift of reason and intellect. They speak and act at my command."

A speck of red flickers in one of his eyes. "Soon, I will create a race that will not live in fear of God, but will rise up and become so pure and divine, God himself will quake on his throne."

"You're sick," I tell him, trembling as I speak. "They tossed you out of school."

Malachai cocks his head. "The old Jew? You saw this? My, Jessamine, you are quite gifted. As for my late . . . professor, he died slowly, as will all his kind."

He pauses, and when he speaks again, his voice is quiet, almost soothing. "I have seen the smoke of a great fire in the distance. One that will cleanse the world of the filth and scum. A new world will arise from the ashes, and it will be made in my image."

"Where is Darby?" I repeat, ignoring him, for I fear his voice might lull me into his web. "What have you done with her?"

"Darby?" he questions. "The servant girl? I will find a use for her. She is quite unique. I have already begun my experiments."

"Mad nutter," Emily whispers.

I gasp. Now is not the time for flippant remarks.

Malachai regards Emily coolly. His lips tighten, like the cruel edge of a blade. A thin thread of red smoke drifts from his forehead and grazes Emily's face. She suddenly bolts upright, and fear blazes in her eyes.

"Dance," Malachai says.

And just like that, Emily begins to do a little jig, a marionette being pulled by strings, small arms and legs bobbing about.

"Stop!" I shout. "You leave her alone!"

"Fascinating, isn't it?" Malachai says. "This power we possess. Sing."

Emily's breath is coming fast, her little dance faltering. She opens her mouth:

"Baa, baa, black sheep, have you any wool? Yes, sir, yes, sir, three bags full—"

"STOP!" I cry out.

"One for the master, one for the dame—"

"Be *still!*" I bellow with all my might.

And Emily crumples to the ground.

There is a moment of silence.

"Interesting," Malachai finally says, looking at me. "You have power you don't even seem to understand."

He takes a step forward. "Come to me, darkling. Come to me, and I will show you how to use that power." He pauses. "The irony is quite interesting, isn't it? To shelter Alexander and Cora's daughter under my wing."

My blood boils.

"I'll never help you," I say through gritted teeth.

He chuckles, and it sounds like flies buzzing in a jar. He reaches into the folds of his jacket and withdraws a small glass vial. Liquid swirls within as he holds it up. *"Yersinia pestis,"* he says proudly. "The Black Death. England first saw it in the thirteenth century. Rats are the perfect vessel for transmission."

In my mind's eye, I see the Rosy Boy, screaming from the vicious bite.

"Even now, I have spread mistrust in the streets, blaming the foreigners and peasants for the sickness. Already they are at each other's throats, like the dogs they are."

Hatred boils in my veins. He is a monster—an evil, wretched creature.

I think of smoke, a powerful white smoke that can choke the life out of the demon in front of me. *Thought made material,* Balthazar called it. If that is true, I need to think of a weapon—something I can use to stop him.

I close my eyes for a brief moment. Immediately I feel it—a warm tingling at my forehead. In an instant, a trail of white smoke floats from my head to Malachai's, but at the same time, a sharp pain stabs me in the stomach, like knives twisting in my gut. I bend in on myself, gasping. I feel as if I will die. My thread of smoke vanishes.

"You have not the strength to compel me, girl," he says.

I'm not going to compel you, I swear to myself. *I'm going to kill you.*

And then Malachai opens his mouth.

I shrink back, for it opens wider than any human mouth should. And out of it pours a smoke so foul and thick, I feel as if I will choke.

Open your mind to me, darkling, I hear inside my head. *Open up and let me in!*

The smoke spills from his mouth and weaves its way toward me. It is full of wriggling shapes and red spots, and makes me think of disease and sickness, a terrible pox.

"If you will not walk with me willingly," Malacahi threatens, "you will walk by my side as an undead thrall."

He steps from the circle. I can smell his breath now, hot and coppery, even though he is several feet away. It has the rot of the grave about it.

His smoke brushes my forehead, and pain sears my stomach again. I close my eyes, trying with all my might to remain standing.

"I am going to take the power from your mind, girl," he hisses. "It will leave you jibbering. Do you know what trepanation is? A small hole is drilled into the skull. Just enough to leave you babbling like the idiot you are, but forever."

A weak light pulses at the edge of my vision. I narrow my eyes to see Emily stirring on the ground. Her light is still pulsing, spilling around her small body. She reaches out a hand to Gabriel, who touches her fingertips.

I hear a sound, faint at first, but steadily growing louder. Something is running—something fast and heavy, with footfalls like drumbeats.

Malachai turns away from me and peers down the tunnel.

A shadow leaps from the darkness.

A tremendous weight knocks me backwards. Sharp claws rip at my clothes. *A ghoul!* I reach out to grapple at the creature's neck, but I don't feel human skin. I feel . . . *fur?*

I look up into wild yellow eyes—eyes like an animal's.

But these eyes I have seen before.

"Darby!" I shout. "Darby. It's me. Jess!"

The creature cocks its wolfish head. *Does she know it's me?* Saliva drips from her teeth.

Malachai's smoke slithers away from my head and coils around the wolf's body. He is trying to compel her.

"Darby!" I shout again, struggling to breathe, for her weight is crushing me. "Your name is *Darby.* Come back to us!"

The wild light seems to fade from her eyes.

And at that moment, as if a clock has just chimed, she scrambles away and lunges at Malachai, knocking him onto his back. His cloud of smoke still clings to her wolf body, winding around her paws and muzzle, but Darby is not hindered. Her snapping jaws are just inches from Malachai's throat.

He is holding her at bay, pressing her neck with his thumbs, trying to keep her jaws from clamping down. I look around for a weapon, something I can use. *Anything!* But there is nothing. Gabriel and Emily rush to my side. Emily's light is pulsing stronger than before. The cut Gabriel suffered is worse than I first thought. The wound looks deep, and blood runs down his face in thin rivulets.

"What do we do?" Emily cries. She looks ready to rush in

and lay hands on Malachai, but I pull her back. "No! It's not safe! You could be slashed."

Slashed, I think. *Like me. Not knowing if you will wake up one day with the skin of a wolf.*

Yet . . . if Darby is a wolf now, it must mean that I am not infected. If so, I would surely be a wolf too.

Gabriel takes a deep breath, and a low sound comes from his throat. My heart races faster. My hands tighten into fists. A surge of energy pulses through my body. Light flickers at Emily's fingers and the ends of her hair.

Malachai throws Darby off, and she crumples against the tunnel wall with a sharp whimper.

"Stupid beast!" he shouts, standing up. He wipes his mouth with the back of his hand and turns to me. His thread of smoke swirls from Darby and streams around my closed mouth. I feel it rising into my nostrils. *I can't breathe!*

Bloodcurdling screams ring through the tunnel.

Ghouls with skull-like faces and red eyes appear from the shadows. They are coming to their master's aid.

"For Brân the Blessed!" Emily shouts, and charges into the oncoming horde. She is dancing between them, her hands a blur of motion, lit up as if aflame, and the ghouls burn like thin parchment at her touch, their corpses dissolving to ash.

"Be at peace, darkling," Malachai says to me. His smoke is curling into my nostrils. I try to breathe again, but my mouth opens and closes like that of a fish on land.

I reflect on the idea of thought made material. I close my eyes and imagine a snake squeezing its prey.

White mist flows from my head—a long, bright cord, and at the end of it, five spiked tails fan out, just like my own lash. I reach up . . .

And my hand closes around it. I can feel it. It is solid. It is *real*.

I do not have time to marvel at it, but only to do one thing.

Within you lies strength yet to be discovered. Like your father . . . and your mother.

I grasp the ethereal whip and strike out.

It curls around Malachai's neck.

Images immediately flood my mind. There is fire and smoke and pain and death. And rats. Always the rats. I am inside his head.

My breath is returning to me. Malachai's smoke is faltering, drifting apart in drops that look like blood.

I hear a vicious snarl, and Darby leaps back into the fray, taking down a ghoul as she does so. The creatures scream and howl, bouncing from wall to wall with amazing speed.

My ribbon of smoke is pulsing now with lines of green and red curling around Malachai's throat. *Tighter!* I shout inside my head. *Tighter!*

Every muscle in my body is strained with exertion,

pushed to the limit. I feel it in my arms and legs, the back of my neck.

Gabriel breathes in, his chest heaves, and then a shadow ripples behind him. I see a shape, outstretched from either side of his small frame.

My mouth falls open.

He lifts his arms, and I see something that shouldn't really exist. A great shadow appears behind him.

Wings.

"Seraph!" Malachai hisses, his hands grasping at my ghostly lash.

The ghouls cower in fear.

"Go back, demon," Gabriel commands. The shadow wings flutter, the edges rippling with fire.

His voice is like rumbling boulders, like trees being wrenched from the very ground. He continues speaking— the words coming faster, a torrent of sound that bears no resemblance to any human language.

The tunnel is now bright with flashing light. Emily is breathing hard, resting with her back to the wall, entranced by Gabriel. The ceiling cracks. Shards of wood and debris crash to the floor, leaving an open hole above. I tumble and roll off the tracks as a plank falls and barely misses my head. I stand up again. My lash of smoke is still tight around Malachai's throat.

But then he is revealed for the devil he truly is.

A serpentine tongue shoots from his mouth. It does not wind its way to me, but to Emily. She falls to the ground, grasping it with her small hands, unable to breathe.

"No!" I scream.

"Release me," he croaks. A slow trickle of black blood oozes from his lips. Red veins appear in his eyes. "Release me, or the girl will die."

I look to Emily. The serpent tongue is curling tighter. Her hands are white-hot, but they do not seem to burn the long, slithering piece of flesh.

Gabriel is singing now. *Or is it the bells?* I can't tell. All I can sense is a *pull* throughout my body. I feel it in my stomach, deep down, like the tide coming into shore. He is calming me.

The silver ship . . . in the faerie realm. Maybe I will go there and be at peace. I will hear Father's song again.

Gabriel's shadow wings begin to glow. A radiance burns around him. His hair blazes with a golden light.

I close my eyes and think of Mother—not the mother with the polite smile and clear green eyes, but the one who lashed out with the whip at 17 Wadsworth Place. The one who battled the power of the dark for years. The one who died for me . . .

I scream.

At the same time, my lash burns a fiery red, and squeezes tighter around Malachai.

His terrible tongue recoils, and Emily lets out a gasping breath. She collapses.

Malachai falls to his knees. "The fire comes!" he wheezes. "The fire will still come!"

In the distance I see a light moving quickly toward us. Hot sparks fly in front of it, dancing in the dark. I feel rushing air on my skin. The tracks beneath my feet begin to hum. My hair floats away from my face. It is closer now, and the sound from my dreams—a terrible screeching and grinding—rings in my ears.

Only then do I realize what it is.

Malachai rises to his feet.

"Emily!" I cry. "Gabriel! Away from the tracks!"

They look to me, and Gabriel drags Emily by her arms toward the tunnel wall.

Malachai turns to look behind him.

The train comes hurtling through the darkness. There is one last scream, and a terrible thumping sound, and then silence.

I stand still. Struck.

I do not want to look at what is left of him. The ghouls are all dead too, their ragged garments still sizzling. Darby slinks off and licks her wounds.

I rush to Emily's side. Her expression is calm, as if she is asleep. I take her by the shoulders. "Emily!" I cry. "Wake up!"

She doesn't stir.

I brush the damp curls away from her face. "Emily, please! *WAKE UP!*"

CHAPTER TWENTY-THREE

Song of Sadness

abriel and I kneel by Emily's body.

I look to him for a brief moment. *Wings?* It can't have been.

He makes the sign of the cross on her forehead.

"Emily," I whisper, taking her hand, cold now. "Emily, don't die." Tears brim in my eyes.

I will lose her, too. Like Mother. And Father.

Gabriel begins to sing softly, and the words—if they are indeed words—fill me with a sense of peace. I hear the rippling of water far away, and wind whistling through treetops. Gabriel sings high, then low. A chorus of voices surrounds him, and it seems so real, I look around for the singers, but it is only the two of us—and Emily, lying asleep, as if she will never awaken.

Gabriel stops his song and leans close to her. He whispers in her ear.

She opens her eyes.

Without a second's pause, I hug her to my chest. She feels as light as a child's dolly.

"Stop," she says weakly.

I loosen my grip. "What is it?" I ask, searching her face for injury. "What's wrong?"

"Bloody crushing me, that's what."

I smile, relieved, and wipe the sweat from her face. Gabriel and I help her rise on unsteady feet. Her lips are dry and cracked. She still needs water.

Gabriel is breathing hard. I think about what I have just seen and heard. What I *think* I have just seen.

Wings.

It must have been just a shadow.

"I am an angel," he says.

I do not speak, only stare.

"There are many of us," he continues. "But we remain hidden, and show ourselves only in times of great need."

"The singing—" I start, without even thinking on what he has just said. "What is it? How do you do it?"

Gabriel pulls out his little book and hands it to me.

I take it, but remain transfixed by his face. I can't believe it. *An angel?* It's impossible.

I shake my head and open the book.

Marks and glyphs seem to writhe on the pages. They are symbols I have never seen before, some of them glowing with a faint golden light, as if they are burned onto the parchment.

"It is Angelica," he says, "the language of angels."

"You can read this?"

"And sing it too. The forces of evil cannot stand the sound of pure love."

Pure love. "That is what gave me strength," I say. "I felt it. In my body."

"Me too," Emily says.

I turn to her. "You knew this? About Gabriel?"

Emily shrugs. "Sorry. He made me promise not to tell."

"Why?" I ask both of them.

"If people knew," Gabriel answers, "I would be sought out and praised. The Church would use me as a symbol. That is not my fate."

This makes sense, I realize. People would flock to him, a living miracle here on earth.

I hear a moan, and I turn, on my guard. *Another ghoul?*

But it is only Darby. She is herself again, lying naked and bruised. I look to Gabriel, who takes off his coat and hands it to me.

I go to Darby and wrap it around her. Livid welts color

her neck. She peers up at me, and I see the crooked teeth, the cold white scars.

"Where are we, miss? Did it happen again?"

"You're safe," I tell her. "You saved us."

She sits up. Her eyes are distant, nervously taking in our surroundings. "Saved you? Where am I? I remember a man. He had terrible eyes. Oh! He was 'orrible, Jess. Just 'orrible!"

Jess. She finally called me Jess.

"Shhh," I whisper, and caress her face. "It's all better now."

She wraps her arms around me and begins to cry.

"Oi, wolf girl," Emily calls weakly. "I think it's time you joined our little club."

CHAPTER TWENTY-FOUR

An Afternoon in the Parlor

Small fires burn in empty trash bins on the High Street, although it is now daybreak.

There is no one in sight but for a few bobbies strolling the alleys. Shiny buttons run the length of their coats, and official badges gleam atop their tall hats. One or two of them look our way, but considering the state we're in—with our dirty, bloody faces and torn clothes—they must take us for a band of guttersnipes.

"Out of here!" they shout, waving their batons and blowing whistles. "The lot of you! Off!"

Several shops are completely destroyed, and broken glass litters the street. Vendors' carts are overturned, their goods scattered and spoiled.

I am supporting most of Emily's weight as we walk, and Gabriel leads Darby, who is still quite dazed and confused. My cheeks burn from the cold, and my fingers are stiff and numb. None of us are dressed properly, seeing as how we rushed out of the house toward a fate we did not know.

But we survived.

And we prevailed. We stopped the evil that was Malachai Grimstead.

Balthazar returns the next day, looking none the worse for wear. We are all sprawled in the parlor and have barely stirred since our return. Darby is curled up by the fire, which I find quite canine-like.

"It's done," I tell him before he has a chance to ask. "Malachai Grimstead. He's dead."

"Again," Emily says.

"Malachai?" Balthazar questions.

"He was behind all of it," I tell him. "From the very beginning. The letter *M*, the sickness, Mother—"

My heart aches.

We tell Balthazar everything: Malachai's rats, his explanation of the word "darkling," my visions of his past, and—strangest of all—the lash I created from my own thoughts.

"Now there is no doubt," he mutters, looking at me curiously.

"No doubt?" I repeat. "Of what?"

But he steers the conversation elsewhere. "Two moons," he says, looking to Darby. "Two moons in one month."

I reach up to touch my scar. Darby had transformed once already. How could it have happened again?

"It is the blue moon," Gabriel says. "A full moon that rises twice in one month, written of in the ecclesiastical calendar."

I look to Gabriel, who is once again the small boy with dark curls and eyes, not the blazing figure I saw in the tunnel. *He is an angel,* I remind myself. *An angel.*

Emily seems better now, after drinking several ewers of water.

I am beyond exhausted, still reeling from the battle. The fire in the grate warms my aching limbs. But finally I ask the question that is weighing on me. "Where were you?" I ask Balthazar. "We needed you." I know I am being rather blunt, but I do not care.

"This was your quest, child," he tells me. "It had to be this way."

I am flabbergasted.

"*My* quest? But what if we were harmed . . . or killed?"

"You swore an oath to this order," he replies without the slightest trace of sentiment.

The words of the initiation come back to me:

And do you swear to use your gift for the good of mankind and strike down evil at any cost, even at risk to your own life?

For a moment, I cannot speak. I hear Emily's breathing deepen and see that she has fallen asleep in her chair. Gabriel's head dips to his chest several times, and he jerks awake, only to let it happen again.

"We all have a great task in life, Jess," Balthazar tells me. "Your parents had theirs in defeating Mephisto, and this was yours—to rise as a member of the League of Ravens, continue their work, and avenge their deaths. You faced a threat brave men would flee from, and that is no small thing."

What Balthazar says is true, and even in this moment, with all that has come to pass, I can think of only one thing: a little girl in Deal, running about the house with a carpet beater as a sword—*The Adventures of Jess the Pirate Girl and her Deeds of Derring-Do!*

Now I have truly seen what adventure holds, and it is no playful lark.

Sleep is a blanket that wraps me in peaceful slumber. There are no dreams of a dark tunnel filled with white mist. I see no man with red eyes or children sick with disease. There is only a deep, restful quiet that embraces my whole being.

And somewhere within that quiet, I see the faces of Mother and Father, who smile upon me and kiss me good night.

CHAPTER TWENTY-FIVE

The Wood Beyond
the World

Darby spills the pile of sticks onto the floor. "Come on, then," she says. "Let's play again."

Emily sighs. "There are other games, you know."

I feel for her, as it is the fourth time they've played, and she seems rather bored.

"But I like *this* game," Darby protests.

Emily sighs again and picks up the sticks.

It has been two days now since our battle in the Underground, and things seem to be returning to normal. That is, if normal is living in a house with a mesmerist, a lightbringer, a werewolf, and an angel. Oh, and a faerie.

We are gathered in the parlor, and while Emily and Darby play jackstraws, I finally gain the courage to ask Gabriel a question that has been plaguing me. I take a breath. "Have you . . . died before?" I ask him. *There. I've said it.* "Do you have to die to become an angel?"

I feel like an absolute beast for prying, but how can I resist? There is an angel in the parlor.

He works on his harp thoughtfully, tightening the little pins that hold the strings in place. "There are things I cannot speak of," he says. "From the world beyond. But I can tell you that death is not the end, Jess. Your mother and father are at rest, and their souls have passed on to a place with no pain or suffering."

These words almost make me weep, but I take another breath and my heart is suddenly filled with a sense of peacefulness. "What will you do now?" I ask him.

He looks at me, and I see that same fierce gaze he wore in battle. "Evil still exists in this world, does it not?"

"Yes."

"That means our work is not yet done. We swore an oath. Remember?"

"Yes," I tell him. "I do remember."

We are interrupted by Balthazar, who strides into the room. He looks to Emily and Darby, and then to me and

Gabriel. He holds a small black box in his hands. *"Ahem,"* he murmurs. "Please. Gather round, if you will."

I rise with a slight pain in my side. The wound from the ghoul is healed, but every now and then I feel a cold, lingering ache. Maybe it will be with me forever, a reminder of the day I avenged my parents.

"Long ago," Balthazar starts, "when the League of Ravens was formed, we worked in the shadows, for that has always been our way. But now a new day has dawned. There is no need to hide, and we should be proud of the work we do, for we hold the line against the dark forces that exist in this world."

He reaches into the box. Cradled within black velvet are several rings. He pulls one out. "Jessamine Grace, wear this ring to show your belief in the power of good over evil, and as a testament to those who have died for our cause."

I take the ring from his hand. It is beautiful, and I know the emblem on the white cameo well—a raven's head surrounded by a wreath of golden leaves. I place it on my finger. "Thank you," I tell him. "It's quite lovely."

He gives Emily and Gabriel their rings. Gabriel takes his without a word, but Emily raises her hand in the air and turns it to and fro, admiringly. "Pretty as a penny, innit?"

I turn to Darby. She should have something too, I realize. After all, without her help, we may not have survived. Fortunately, Balthazar seems to think the same.

"As for you, Darby," he begins, "you have shown great courage in defeating a foe that many would flee from. Do you wish to relinquish your role as servant and serve a greater cause?"

Darby looks to me and then back to Balthazar. She opens her mouth but closes it again. Emily nudges her with an elbow. "C'mon, wolf girl," she says. "Time to hang up that apron, yeah?"

Darby smiles, revealing her crooked teeth. "Yes, sire," she says. "I'd like that very much."

Balthazar leans forward and looks her in the eye. "It's Balthazar," he says with a smile.

He straightens up and tugs at his waistcoat. "Well then," he continues. "Jessamine. I believe you know what comes next."

And I do.

I retrieve the spear from the corner of the room. And as we draw the curtains and initiate Darby into our order, I realize that there is no place I'd rather be.

I find Balthazar in the parlor the next morning, eating a pomegranate. I watch closely to see if he truly does eat, but he interrupts my spying by sliding a newspaper across the table. My eyes scan the page and land on a curious article:

THE DAILY TELEGRAPH & COURIER

Man Dies in Underground

An unidentified man has died in a disturbance in the newly constructed Underground. Scotland Yard reports that the man's death came during a trial run of trains operating on the South Eastern Railway's Paddington to Farrington route.

Several piles of smoldering ash, which emit a foul odor, have also been found at the scene. The tunnel roof was destroyed, and inspectors are not certain of the cause. Anyone with information as to the dead man's identity, or the mysterious ash, is urged to come forward to their local constable.

I raise my eyes to Balthazar. "They'll never really know, will they? That a creature of the underworld was in their midst, sending the city into madness and death."

"No, they will not, Jessamine, and I am certain they are better off not knowing."

I imagine what the scene must have looked like in the aftermath—debris and smoke, and the ash, which was certainly the remains of the undead ghouls.

Balthazar scoots his chair back from the table. "Come,"

he says. "Fetch a cloak. There is something I would like to show you."

I wonder what it could be. At this point, nothing would surprise me.

We take a hansom cab, and I am lulled by the rhythm of the ride—the creaking wheels and the clip-clop of horses' hooves. The cold air on my face is pleasant and relaxing.

We exit the carriage on the edge of a wood. It strikes me as odd, for the forest looms at what seems to be the dead end of a street and looks quite out of place, almost as if it is a painting, or what the French call *trompe l'oeil*, a trick of the eye, an expression I recall from my governess.

Two trees stand opposite each other, and the boughs that rise overhead form an arch, providing a sort of entrance. I pause. "Where are you taking me?"

"Not much farther," he says as we step into the wood.

The forest floor is damp, and the musky scent of mushrooms and loamy soil rises in my nostrils. Cool winter sunlight filters through the bare tree branches. It is quiet here; not even the sound of birds can be heard. We are silent for several minutes, with only the sound of our footsteps. "Do you remember the verse?" Balthazar asks.

"Verse?" I venture, confused.

"The one I recited upon first meeting you. 'Long ago, in the early days of the world . . .'"

I nod my head and open my mouth before realizing I am doing so. "'When man still walked among the ancient groves.'"

Unusual that I would remember that. Then again, I have always been good at rhymes and such, and recall to this day the silly stories Mother recited when I was a child.

"'And every doorstep led to a lush green meadow,'" Balthazar continues.

And I join him: "'Men and women often visited the Twilight Folk, and with leaves in their hair, danced in dizzying circles.'"

"'To the trill of the flute and the beat of the drum,'" Balthazar adds. "'To fall into a deep reverie under a thousand twinkling stars.'"

My head is light on my shoulders. The forest suddenly seems more alive. I almost feel as if the ground beneath my feet is moving. I open my mouth again, and the words fall out before I can even think. "'Only to awake to find themselves entwined in an embrace, Fae and mortal bound together.'"

Balthazar stops walking. He turns to me, and I swear that his eyes are now golden, flecked with green. The hair on the nape of my neck stirs.

"Why do I remember that?" I ask. "How?"

He takes my gloved hands in his bare ones. "Because you, my child . . . you are of the faerie folk."

I don't speak. The slight wind stirs the dead leaves around my feet. I need to steady myself. I turn away from him and reach out to a tree for support.

"I first suspected it when you were scratched by Darby," he says. "You healed quickly, Jess. Too quickly for someone wholly human. I took the blood from your handkerchief to what my kind call the Shining Court. There it was studied. They needed proof, you see, that you were indeed half fae."

He stops and grins. "The rules and formalities in Faerie make Britain seem a country backwater."

My hand is still resting on the tree. The rough bark seems to be wriggling beneath my fingers. *Me? Half fae?*

"That was why I was away after Darby's attack," he continues, "and why I could not join you at your very hour of need. When you set out for Mephisto, the Shining Court called a conclave at the exact same time. I had no choice but to be there. And it was all about you, my child."

I stare out into the distance, still not looking at Balthazar. A deer pauses and studies us, then leaps away silently. Finally I turn to him. "And what of it?" I ask. "This conclave."

The light around Balthazar seems to shimmer. "There is no doubt, child. You possess the blood."

"But how?" I ask. "Mother—"

"Cora was indeed human. But your *father* . . ."

My heart skips. "What?" I ask. "What of Father?"

Balthazar lets out a weary breath. "Your mother would want you to know, Jess, but she was never really sure."

"Sure of what?" I ask, eager now. *More secrets. They never end.* "What would she want me to know?"

"Your father, Alexander Grace, was of the royal blood, what we call the Tuatha Dé Danann."

The words are lyrical, and they flow from Balthazar's lips like rippling water.

"His lineage goes back for generations, and now you, too, can claim this bloodline."

Images of Father float in my mind—his tall, slender build, the gray eyes so light they looked almost silver, his love of nature, and our walks in the botanical gardens.

"We were young then," Balthazar says, and his expression softens, "your mother, father, and I. Such days. . . ."

He trails off, and there is a note of melancholy in his voice.

"They fell in love, Alexander and your mother. But my people—your father's people—did not approve."

"But wait—" I start. "The verse. It says that men and women often visited the Twilight Folk—"

Balthazar smiles ruefully. "There have been times when my kind enchanted the mortal folk, more of a foolish whim than anything else. But your parents' love was greater than that, and it was kept secret, amidst the whispering trees at night. Your father was of the royal blood,

Jess. The Shining Court would not abide for someone of his rank to wed a human."

A bird alights on a branch above my head and chirrups loudly.

"Not every child born of fae and human blood is graced with the faerie bloodline, Jessamine. You, like me, are blessed to be of both worlds. Do you remember the painting? The one at SummerHall?"

A memory comes to me. A large painting above the hearth at Balthazar's estate: a woman with lustrous black hair running through a forest. *Her name was Lady Estella*, he had said. *A faerie maiden who was in love with a mortal man.*

"Your . . . mother?" I ask tentatively.

"Yes," he replies.

"So we're alike?" I venture. "You and me?"

"We are, my child. Your mother suspected, but never really knew. Now we are certain."

We begin to walk once more. My legs are unsteady. Balthazar offers his arm, and I loop mine through his. There is something else that comes to me, something he never explained. "The lash—" I begin. "I lost my weapons in the tunnel and at the last minute summoned a lash from my own thoughts."

We stop, and he turns to me.

"Just one more example of who you are," he says. "You are truly gifted with the power of my people."

I let out a tremulous breath. This little walk of ours has revelations at every step.

We reach a small circle of trees, and Balthazar pauses. "Why are we stopping here?" I ask.

"You are standing on a faerie ring," he says.

I look down to see a small mound of green, about a foot high, ringed by yellow wildflowers and pale, spotted mushrooms. "Oh," I say.

"Close your eyes," Balthazar says, stepping onto the mound with me.

"Why?" I ask him.

"I want to show you something—something you wanted to see again."

I know what it is, as surely as I know my own name. "The silver ship?" I ask.

But he doesn't answer, and only closes his own eyes.

The trees seem to blur around us. I feel the earth beneath my feet moving. Far away, as if it is coming from these very woods, I hear a refrain, and it is one that I have heard before:

The smile upon her bonnie cheek was sweeter than the bee . . .

I close my eyes.

And then there is only the sound of rushing air and the peculiar sensation of falling.

The End

ACKNOWLEDGMENTS

I did a lot of research for this book, and various materials helped me bring Jess and her Victorian England to life. An old copy of Bradshaw's *Handbook for Tourists in Great Britain & Ireland* was very helpful with train schedules and distances. *Dirty Old London: The Victorian Fight Against Filth* by Lee Jackson also provided much inspiration. During my research, I came across a PDF of a rare, long-out-of-print book called *Street Life in London,* written by Adolphe Smith and with photographs by John Thomson. The book is a delight, and the black-and-white photographs helped fire my imagination.

Thanks to everyone at Clarion Books/Houghton Mifflin Harcourt for their enthusiasm and support of this book. My editor, Lynne Polvino, who asked all the right questions, along with Lisa Vega, Dinah Stevenson, Karen Walsh, Lisa DiSarro, Tara Shanahan, Amanda Acevedo, and everyone behind the scenes who had a hand in getting *The Mesmerist* out into the world.

Of course, I wouldn't be here without the support of my Super Agent, Adriann Ranta. Thanks for your patience and guidance.

I'd also like to thank Lisa K. Weber for the great cover. The Children's Bookstore in Baltimore, Maryland, has been a great supporter. Thank you, JoAnn Fruchtman, Rachel Machesky, and the entire staff.

All writers need cheerleaders, and the folks at Politics and Prose Bookstore have been incredible. Thank you.

Michele Thornton, for your feedback, your support, and being a good friend.

Thanks to the Smith and Sofio clans as well as the Robinson women for their endless championing of my work.

Julia, you're last, but always first. You deserve endless chocolate. And a buttery croissant.